Shapes that Haunt the Dusk

𝕳arper's 𝕹ovelettes

EDITED BY
WILLIAM DEAN HOWELLS
AND
HENRY MILLS ALDEN

Harper & Brothers Publishers
New York and London

Introduction

THE writers of American short stories, the best short stories in the world, surpass in nothing so much as in their handling of those filmy textures which clothe the vague shapes of the borderland between experience and illusion. This is perhaps because our people, who seem to live only in the most tangible things of material existence, really live more in the spirit than any other. Their love of the supernatural is their common inheritance from no particular ancestry, but is apparently an effect from psychological influences in the past, widely separated in time and place. It is as noticeable among our Southerners of French race as among our New-Englanders deriving from Puritan zealots accustomed to wonder - working providences, or among those descendants of the German immigrants who brought with them to our Middle States the supersti-

tions of the Rhine valleys or the Hartz
Mountains.   It is something that has
tinged the nature of our whole life, whatever its varied sources, and when its color
seems gone out of us, or, going, it renews
itself in all the mystical lights and shadows so familiar to us that; till we read
some such tales as those grouped together here, we are scarcely aware how
largely they form the complexion of our
thinking and feeling.

The opening story in this volume is
from a hand quite new, and is, we think,
of an excellence quite absolute, so fresh
is it in scene, character, and incident,
so delicately yet so strongly accented by
a talent trying itself in a region hardly
yet visited by fiction.   Its perfect realism
is consistent with the boldest appeal to
those primitive instincts furthest from
every-day events, and its pathos is as
poignant as if it had happened within
our own knowledge.   In its way, it is as
finely imaginative as Mr. Pyle's wonder-
fully spiritualized and moralized concep-
tion of the other world which he has realized on such terms as he alone can command; or as Mrs. Wynne's symphony of
thrills and shudders, which will not have
died out of the nerves of any one ac-
quainted with it before.   Mr. Millet's

sketch is of a quality akin to that of Mr. McVickar's slighter but not less impressive fantasy: both are "in the midst of men and day," and command such credence as we cannot withhold from any well-confirmed report in the morning paper. Mr. Rice's story is of like temperament, and so, somewhat, is Miss Hawthorne's, and Mr. Brown's, and Miss Bradley's, while Miss Davis's romance is of another atmosphere, but not less potent, because it comes from farther, and wears a dreamier light.

Such as they severally and differently and collectively are, the pieces are each a masterpiece and worthy the study of every reader who feels that there are more things than we have dreamt of in our philosophy. The collection is like a group of immortelles, gray in that twilight of the reason which Americans are so fond of inviting, or, rather, they are like a cluster of Indian pipe, those pale blossoms of the woods that spring from the dark mould in the deepest shade, and are so entirely of our own soil.

W. D. H.

The Christmas Child

BY GEORG SCHOCK

THE moonlight was so bright across the clock that it showed the time, and its tick was solemn, as though the minutes were marching slowly by. There was no other sound in the room except the breathing of Conrad, who lay in shadow, sleeping heavily, his head a black patch among the pillows. Mary's hair looked like gold in the pale light which reflected in her open eyes. She had been lying so, listening to the tick and watching the hands, for hours.

When they marked eleven she began to stir; her feet made no more sound than shadows; the cold air struck her body like a strange element. Conrad did not move as she went into the kitchen and softly closed the door. She groped her way to the chair where she had left her clothes and put them on, wrapped herself in a shawl, and slipped out. S. H. D.

There was no snow, but a keen cold as befitted the night of the 24th of December, and between two fields the ice on the Northkill glittered. The air was so clear that far away appeared the great black barrier of the mountains. Across the sky, as across deep water, was a radiance of light, serene and chill,— of clouds like foam, of throbbing stars, of the moon glorious in her aura. In the towns at that hour the people were ready to begin the coming day with prayer and the sound of bells: here sky and earth themselves honored the event with light and silence in a majestic expectation.

As she made her way over the frozen grass she looked as detached from the world's affairs as some shrouded lady at her nightly journey along a haunted path. The great Swiss barn was dead silent; its red front, painted with moons and stars, looked patriarchal; it had its own pastoral and dignified associations. She hesitated at the middle door, then she lifted the wooden bar and pushed it back cautiously. The darkness seemed to come out to meet her, and when she had shut herself in she was engulfed as though the ready earth had covered her a few nights too soon.

The straw rustled when she stepped on it, and she was afraid to risk a movement, so she crouched and made herself small. The air was thick and pungent, freezing draughts played upon her through the cracks of the door, and her foot tingled, but she did not move. After a while she saw two luminous disks which halted, glared, and approached, and she patted the furry body until it curled up on her skirt and lay there purring. She felt it grow tense at a tiny squeak and scuttle, but she kept still.

More than half an hour had gone when something happened. A horse stamped, a cock set up a sudden chatter, the cat leaped to a manger, and a cow scrambled to her feet. The darkness was full of movement, — wings fluttered, timbers shook under kicking hoofs and rubbing hides, tossed heads jarred the rings that held them fast. Then from the corner in which stood the splendid yoke of black oxen, the pride of the farm, there came a long, deep sound, as of something primeval mourning.

Two minutes after, Conrad was roused by a noise in the kitchen. The house door stood wide, showing a great rectangle of moonlight, there was a rush of

cold air, and his bare foot struck Mary,
doubled up where she had fallen. He
shouted, and an old woman ran in with
her gray hair flying.

"Conrad!" she exclaimed, almost in a
scream.

"I don't know," he answered. He had
his wife in his arms and held her out
like a child showing a broken toy.

The old woman bethought herself first.
"Take her in and lay her on the bed,"
she ordered. While she worked he began
to hurry on his clothes, moving as though
he were stupid; then he came up to the
bed.

"Aunt Hannah, what has she?" he
begged. She gave him a look, and he
suddenly burst into a great storm of
tears.

"Hurry!" she said. "Take Dolly and
a whip and go to Bernville first. If the
doctor isn't home, go along to Mount
Pleasant; but bring a doctor. Ach!"
she seized his hand in her excitement.

Mary's eyes were opening—blue, wide,
and terrified. "Don't take Dolly," she
said, quite loud. "Dolly knows too
much." Then her eyes closed again.

Conrad went into the kitchen, still
sobbing, and the old woman followed.

"I must take Dolly," he whispered.

"Aunt Hannah, for God's sake, what has she?"

"I don't know what she means about Dolly. Maybe I can find out till you get back. She'll soon come to. You better be careful going out of the barnyard. It might worry her if she hears the hoofs."

The young man checked his crying. "I take her through the fields," he said, and went out softly.

In the light of the candle which contended with the moonbeams Hannah's wrinkled face looked witchlike as she bent over the bed. Presently Mary started and her eyes searched the room with a terrified stare; she seemed to be all at once in the midst of some dreadful happening.

"Aunt Hannah," she exclaimed, "don't let them come for me!"

The old woman bent over her. "How do you feel?" she asked, in her soft and friendly Dutch.

"Don't let them come!"

"Nobody comes, Mary. It is all right, only you are not so good. After while somebody is coming. Then you are glad!"

"Keep them out! I don't want to go!"

"You don't go off; you stay right here with me and Conrad."

"They said—"

"Who?"

"The oxen."

Hannah's hand shook, but she still spoke reassuringly. "Were you in the barn, Mary?"

"Yes. You know how it is said that on Christmas eve, twelve o'clock, the animals talk. I thought so much about it, and I made up my mind to go and hear what they had to say. I was in the middle stable that's empty, and I waited, and all of a sudden—" She stopped, trembling.

"Just don't think about it," Hannah urged, but she went on:

"All of a sudden—Dolly stamped—and they all woke up—the cows and the sheep, and the cat was scared and the big rooster cackled,—and then the oxen—Ach, Aunt Hannah! One of them said, 'They will carry out the mistress in the morning.'"

"You don't go, for all," the old woman soothed her. "Think of who is coming, Mary. That's a better thing to think about. It's so lucky to have it on Christmas day. She will have good fortune then, and see more than others."

The pinched face grew bright. The trembling soul was not to go out alone before, becoming a part of the great current of maternity, it had had the best of what is here.

"I take such good care of her. I look after her all the time," said Mary.

The sun was gone, but the west was still as pink as coral and the twilight gave a wonderful velvety look to the meadows. In the rye-fields the stalks, heavy-headed already, dipped in the wind which blew the last apple-blossoms about like snow. A row of sturdy trees grew along Conrad Rhein's front fence, and there was a large orchard in the rear. The log house was just the color of a nest among the pale foliage.

The place was so quiet that the irritable note of a couple of chimney-swallows, swooping about in pursuit of an invisible purpose, sounded loud. Hannah Rhein looked up from the small stocking she was knitting to watch them. Her secular occupation was contradicted by her black silk "Sunday dress," and there was a holiday appearance about the little girl who sat very still, looking as though stillness were habitual with her.

"You better run out to the gate. Maybe you can see them," Hannah said.

The child went, and stood looking down
the road so long that she rolled up her
knitting and followed. " There they are !"
she exclaimed. " Father and Aunt Calista. Don't forget to give her a kiss
when she gets out."

Conrad Rhein's austere face expressed
no pleasure as he stepped from the carriage and helped his companion, but she
was not to be depressed by a brother-in-
law's gravity. Calista Yohe, moving
lightly in her pink delaine dress, resem-
bled the prickly roses coming into bloom
beside the gate, which would flourish and
fade imperturbably in accordance with
their own times and seasons. At present
she looked as though the fading were
remote. She shook hands joyfully and
seized the carpet-bag which Hannah had
taken.

" I guess I don't let you carry that,"
she said. " It's heavy."

The little girl put up her face, and
Calista kissed her without speaking to
her, and went on talking:

" You are right, Dolly is hot. We
drove good and hard. Conrad didn't
want to do it to give her the whip, but
I don't like to ride slow. Let's sit on
the porch awhile."

The child placed her bench near the

old woman's chair, but she watched the young one admiringly. Calista did not notice her.

"How are the folks?" Hannah asked.

"They are good."

"Had they a big wedding?"

"I guess! It was teams on both sides of the road all the way down to where you turn, and they had three tables. She wore such a nice dress, too; such a silk it was, with little flowers in."

"How did it go while you were there?"

"Oh, all right; she's a nice girl and he and I could always get along; but it wasn't like my home. If a man gets married once, he doesn't want his sister afterwards," Calista said, cheerfully.

"Well, you stay here now. We are glad to have you. Conrad he is quiet and I am getting along, so it's not such a lively place, but I guess you can make out."

"Well, I think!" said Calista. "I like to work. Is Conrad always so crabbed? He hardly talked anything all the way over."

"He hasn't much to say, but he is easy to get along with. He doesn't look much to anything but the farm."

"Doesn't he go out in company?" Calista asked, eagerly.

"Once in a while, but not often. He doesn't look for that any more." Hannah sighed and stroked the child's head, which rested against her knee, and the movement caught Calista's eye.

"She favors Mary," she said. "All that light hair and her white skin. That's a pretty dress she has on." She stooped and examined the blue merino. "Did you work that sack?"

"No, I had it worked. I think she looks nice. Conrad bought her those blue beads for a present. She was so glad."

"Does she always wear white stockings?"

"When she is dressed. Conrad he wants it all of the best."

"Does he think so much of her?"

"He doesn't make much with her; he is not one to show if he thinks much; but would be strange if he didn't. And as well off as he is, and no one to spend it on!"

Calista looked out through the orchard and across the fields of rye and wheat over which the spring night was falling. "He has a fine place for sure," she said. "He takes long in the barn."

"I guess he went off," said Hannah, peacefully.

"I didn't see him leave."

" It may be he went to Albrecht's."

" Who are they? Young people?"

" Yes. John Albrecht he is about Conrad's age, and his wife was such a friend to Mary. They have two little ones come over sometimes to play around."

" Is that all in the family?"

" His mother; she lives with her, a woman so crippled up she can't walk."

Calista looked as satisfied as a strategist who finds himself in control of a desired situation: its difficulties made her spirits rise. Her eyes wandered about and fixed upon the child again. " She gets sleepy early for such a big girl," she said. " Wasn't she five on Christmas?"

" Yes. She wanted to see you, so I let her stay up to-night; and anyhow I didn't want to be sitting up-stairs when you got here."

" Do you sit with her evenings?"

" Till she goes to sleep. If you leave her in the dark she is so scared I pity her, and I don't want her to get excited. I have no trouble with her other times. She listens to me, and she is real smart to help; she can pick strawberries and pull weeds, and she always enjoys to go along for eggs. She is like her father, she hasn't much to say. She will run around in the orchard and play with her

doll-baby the whole day, and she is pretending all the time."

The little girl opened her eyes, very
blue with sleep. With her rosy color and
the white and blue of her little garments
she looked like a cherub smiling out of the
canvas of a German painter,—the soft
companion of an older and more pensive
grace. Hannah watched her tenderly.

"Now come, Mary, we go to bed," she
said.

"I guess I'd make such a fuss with
that child and sit with her nights!" Calista thought, her prominent hazel eyes
following in rather a catlike fashion.
They followed in the same way more
than once during the next few weeks.
She would brush the little girl's hair
when Hannah was busy, or call her to a
meal, but at other times she passed her
by. At first Mary was inclined to pursue
the pretty stranger, and on the second
evening she ran up to her to show the
results of the egg-hunting, but she never
did it again.

She was the only one whom Calista
failed to please. The neighbors who
came to visit soon returned, and on
Saturday night there were three car-
riages at the gate and three young men
in the parlor. Conrad did not pay much

attention to her, but one day he told her
that one of her admirers was "not such
a man that you ought to go riding with,"
and she said: "All right. It was two
asked me to go to-night. I take the other
one." She went through the work singing, and Hannah sat on the porch more
than usual, and began to wonder how she
had gotten on so long alone.

Calista had been there only a few
weeks, when Hannah said at supper one
evening: "I guess I go to see your aunt
Sarah, Conrad. It's six years since I
went. I couldn't leave the work before,
but now Calista gets along so good I can
go a little."

"Just do it," said Calista, heartily.
"Mary and I can keep house."

The child smiled and made a timid
movement.

"All right," Conrad said. "I take
you to the stage any time."

Mary cried when Hannah went, and
the old woman was distressed. "I feel
bad to leave her," she said. "I would
take her along if I had time to get her
ready."

"Ach, go on!" Calista said, laughing.
"There is Conrad now with the team.
Mary will have good times. She can
stem the cherries this morning." She

picked up the little girl and held her out
to kiss her aunt. "Don't you worry,"
she called, as the carriage started.

She came out on the back porch
presently with a large basket of
ox-hearts.

"Now let's see how smart you can be,"
she said. "Sit down on the step and I
put the basket beside you. Pick them
clean." Mary looked rather frightened
at the size of the task, but she set to
work. She stemmed and stemmed until
her hands were sticky and her fingers
ached. A thick yellow sunbeam came
crawling to her feet; the flies buzzed,
diving through the air as though it were
heavy; the cat beside her slept and woke.
It seemed to the child that she had always
been in that spot and that there would
never be anything but a hot morning
and piles of shining cherries. She was
looking toward the orchard where her
swing hung empty when Calista hurried
by the door. "Have you done them all?"
she called. "Not? Well, then you finish them quick."

The cherries lasted until dinner-time,
and when that was over Mary climbed
on her father's bed and slept all afternoon. When she came out the first thing
she saw was the egg-basket piled full,

"If you want to go along for eggs you ought to be here when I am ready," said Calista.

The little creature made no noise, but her father looked at her hard as he sat down to supper. "What's the matter?" he asked.

She did not answer, and Calista said, "Oh—!" with the peculiar German inflection of contemptuous patience. Conrad said no more.

After supper Mary wandered out, and her aunt had to call her several times. "Where were you?" she asked.

"Down there." The child pointed to the orchard. "A lady was there."

Calista went to the edge of the porch and shaded her eyes. "I don't see her," she said. "Who was she?"

"I don't know."

"Did you never see her before?"

"No, ma'am."

"What did she look like?"

Mary thought hard, with the puzzled face of one who lacks words and comparisons to convey an image that is clear enough. Calista walked a little way into the orchard, then she looked up and down the road.

"Wasn't it Mrs. Albrecht?" she asked. "Well, I guess it makes nothing. Come,

you must go to bed. I stay with you."
With a mocking expression she held out
her hand as to a very small child, and
the little girl walked into the house without a word, not noticing the hand.

When she was asleep Calista came back
to the porch with some sewing. Conrad
appeared from the barn, stood about for
a moment, and strolled toward the orchard; then he walked in the garden
for a while; finally he sat on the step
with his back to her, saying nothing and
looking at the sky. She preserved the
silence of a bird-tamer.

"It's a nice evening," he said at last.

"Yes."

"Good weather for hay."

"Yes, fine."

"One field is about ready to cut. You
better tell Aunt Hannah to come home.
It's too much work for you, with the
men to cook for."

"Just you let her stay and enjoy herself. I get along all right."

After a pause she asked, "Did you
see some one in the orchard just now?"

"No."

"Mary she ran down after supper, and
she said a strange lady was there. I
wondered who it was."

"I didn't see her," he said, dully, as

though he spoke from the midst of some absorbing thought; then he got up and walked away. "You better go in and light the lamp if you want to sew," he said, roughly.

Calista took her things and went at once, looking as though she were so well satisfied that she could afford to be amused.

Though in the next two weeks she had plenty of company Conrad never joined them: he spent the evenings with John Albrecht, drove to Bernville, or went to bed early. He worked much harder than usual, and his cheeks grew thin under his stubble of black beard. Calista did not trouble him with conversation.

"Don't you feel good?" she once asked, and when he gave a surly answer she said, carelessly, "You better get something from the doctor," and began to sing immediately afterwards. But she knew how he looked even when her back was turned, and she often stared at Mary in a meditative way as though the child were the doubtful quantity in an important calculation.

She was watching her so one day, when little John Albrecht and his sister had come over and the three were very busy on the grass near the kitchen window

with two dolls and the old tiger-cat. In
the afternoon silence their little voices
sounded clear and sweet. The cat escaped to a cherry-tree and they chased
him gayly, but he went to sleep in an
insulting way in spite of the lilac switch
that John flourished.

"Look out!" Mary called.

John looked around and said, "For
what?" and she went over to him.

There was a conversation which Calista
could not hear; Mary pointed several
times to a spot in the sunny grass; then
he went running down the road and
Katie followed, looking as though she
would cry when she had time, and leaving
her doll behind her.

Calista went out. "What did you say
to John to make them run off?" she asked.

"I told him to look out, he would hit
the lady with the switch."

"What lady?"

"She was there."

"Where is she now?"

"I don't know."

"Can't you see her?"

"No, ma'am."

Calista looked all about. Not a soul
was in sight on the road; in the orchard
and the fields nothing moved but the
wind; the yard was empty except for the

cat slipping around the corner with his mottled coat shining. "Now listen," she said, not unkindly. "I saw you out of the window, and there was no lady here. Why do you tell a story like that?"

The child looked at her in a preoccupied way and did not answer.

"I can't have you say things that are not so, Mary. If you do it again, I have to whip you. Now pick up your doll-baby and come in."

She spoke of it to Conrad that evening, but he did not pay much attention.

"I don't know if there is something wrong with Mary or, if she does see some one, who it is," she said. "Do you know if there are gipsies around?" He scarcely answered, and in a few minutes she heard him drive down the road. She smiled to herself as she hurried through her work. Then she put Mary to bed, though it was much earlier than usual, and began to dress, while the little girl lay watching from among the pillows.

Calista enjoyed the water like a sleek creature of two elements; her white skirts crackled and flared; her hair hid her waist. When she had finished her green dimity looked like foliage around a flower, and her hazel eyes turned green to match it.

"I'm going on the front porch," she
said. "You go to sleep like a good girl."

She had sat with Mary in the evening
as long as she could do so without in-
convenience. Now she saw no reason for
continuing it. She had not imagination
enough to know what she was inflicting.
Mary gazed after her as a shipwrecked
woman might watch a plank drifting out
of reach, but she said nothing; she shut
her eyes and lay still for many minutes.
She was a timid child but not cowardly,
and such tangible things as a cross dog,
a tramp, and a blacksnake in the orchard
she had faced bravely, but her terror of
the dark was indefinite and unendurable.
She opened her eyes, shut them, and
opened them again, looking for something dreadful. The furniture was shape-
less, the bedclothes dimly white, and each
time she looked it was darker. She did
not know what she expected, and to see
nothing was almost worse. A carriage
going down the road comforted her as
long as she could hear it, but it left a
thicker silence. She pressed her lids together, breathing quickly,—to move was
like inviting something to spring on her,
—then she slid out of bed and ran down
the stairs, gave a frightened glance at
the front door behind which sat her aunt,

who would send her up again, and slipped
across the back porch into the orchard.

Calista heard nothing. In the hot
June evening she was fresh and cool
enough to be akin to the rejoicing fields,
a nymph of beech or willow. Now and
then she looked down the road and saw
no one, but she did not seem disappointed.
It was quite dark and the fireflies were
trailing up and down when wheels
stopped at the gate, and she drew back
behind a lilac-bush that screened the
porch, and sat still.

Conrad, striding up the path, started
when he saw her. "Oh, it's you!" he
said, coldly. She gave a short answer,
and he stood frowning at nothing and
looking very tall and black. "Want to
take a little ride?" he asked.

"No, I guess not."

"You stay at home too much," he said,
presently. "You haven't been off the
place since Aunt Hannah left."

"I don't care to go. I can't leave Mary
here all alone. It wouldn't be safe."

She stayed silently in her corner as
though waiting for him to leave—a white
shadow beside the black mass of the lilac-
bush. Dolly at the gate tossed her head
until the reins scraped on the gate-post.
Down in the orchard a whippoorwill cried.

He was like a horse that takes the bit
and the driver was' his own will—his
own self. She made no resistance when
he threw himself down beside her: she
was pliant, her cheek cool, she even looked
at him haughtily. He did not know that
she slipped out of his arms just before
he would have released her, nor that she
'was all one flame of triumphant happiness. She seemed as untouched as the
starlight.

"Calista," he stammered, "I hope you
overlook it."

"What about my sister Mary?" she
asked, dryly. "I thought you didn't look
to any one else."

"I didn't. I tell you the truth. I
was unwilling. I fought it off all I could,
but now I give in. I can do no more."

"So you think you like me as well as
you like her?"

"Calista, I would ask you if Mary
stood here and heard us."

The woman seemed to bloom like an
opening rose. She looked at him, but
it was as though she saw some vision of
success that she was just about to grasp.
"I am satisfied," she said.

There was a sound on the walk, and
they lifted their heads; then they were
scarcely conscious of each other's pres-

ence. Up from the gate, her night-
dress hanging about her feet, her hair
pale in the dim light, came the little
girl. She climbed the steps and passed
fearlessly into the dark house, smiling
at the two with the radiant content of
happy childhood, soothed and petted,—
her small right hand held up as if in the
clasp of another hand.

Calista would have chosen to clean the
whole house or do a harvest-time baking
rather than write one letter, so she asked
most of the guests verbally and put off the
others as long as she could. Conrad had
taken Hannah to Bernville to have a
new silk dress fitted and buy colored
sugar for the wedding-cakes when she
began the invitations. By three o'clock
they were finished, and she counted them
and laid them beside the inkstand. Then
she washed her hands, spread a sheet on
the floor, and got out a pile of soft white
stuff, all puffs and lace and ruffles—the
work of weeks.

She sewed happily, looking out now
and then at the trees, which tossed like
green waves under the roaring August
rain. Sometimes a gust drove a shower
down the chimney and made the logs
hiss. The room was warm and still; in

the interval of work it seemed to have
paused and be sleeping. The tiger-
cat, with his paws folded under him, lay
beside the hearth, and Mary on her little
bench nursed her doll peacefully. Calista
began to sing a German hymn; the words
were awful, but their very solemnity
made her happier by contrast:

" Wer weiss wie nahe mir mein Ende!
  Hin geht die Zeit, her kommt der Tod.

"Look here, Mary," she said. "Isn't
this pretty?" The child came, and Calista held up the soft stuff around her;
it made the little face look beautifully
pink and white. She touched it lightly,
smiling, then she wandered over to the
window with her doll and looked out into
the rain.

" Es kann vor Nacht leicht anders werden,
  Als es am frühen Morgen war,"

Calista sang.
    Five minutes later she asked, good-
naturedly, "What are you looking at?"
Mary did not answer. "Didn't you hear
what I said? What's going on out
there?" Calista repeated.
    "You said I shouldn't say it," the child
whispered.
    "Say what?"

"When I see the lady."

"Where do you see her?"

"Coming out of the orchard."

Certain old stories returning to Calista's mind made her look at Mary for a minute as though the child had manifested strange powers. She went to the window and her thimble clicked on the sill as she leaned forward; then she touched her cheek. "Do you feel good?" she asked.

"Yes, ma'am."

She looked out again. "I want you to know for sure that no one is there," she said, earnestly. "Now tell me: do you see a lady?"

"Yes, ma'am. She is coming up here."

Calista was very sober. "If your aunt Hannah doesn't teach you not to tell stories, then I must," she said. "I can't have you like this. Soon I can't believe you anything. Come here." Mary came as if pulled. "Now mind, I do this so that you don't say what isn't so again." She gave the child two good slaps on the mouth with her strong hand.

The inherited spirit of resistance to coercion, that had made pioneers and martyrs of Mary Rhein's ancestors, was let loose too soon: it made an imp of

her. She darted silently like an insect
from under Calista's hand, seized the
inkstand, and threw it with all her
might at the beautiful white gown. The
ink poured out, dripping from fold to
fold, and the stand thudded on the sheet
and scattered the last drops. Mary gave
one look and ran across the porch and
out to the road in the rain.

Calista sat still for a moment, then
she got up weakly. "Doesn't look much
like a wedding-dress now," she murmured. "It's no use doing anything to
it. It's done for." She wiped the inkstand on a stained flounce before setting it on the table. "*Now*," she said,
as though some one were present who
would disapprove, "I give it to her good.
I better fetch her in and have it done
before they get back."

The sky was low but the rain was gentle when she started down the road, and
her shawl made a bright spot between the
fields, green as chromos. Mary had gone
toward the creek, and she followed as far
as the bridge; then, as there was no one
in sight, she turned up-stream. It was
deep just there and very full, carrying
leaves and twigs so that it was like
a little flood, and the water caught the
dipping branches of the willows and

swept them along. The shellbarks looked
forlorn in the rain, and the ground was
so soft that it gave under her feet. Her
skirts and shoes were heavy with wet
before she saw Mary.

The child looked as though she were
being crowded out of life. She was crying, with small weak sounds like a wretched little animal, her hair was dark with
water, and the rain drove across her face.
At the sight of Calista she began to run
slowly with much stumbling; her crying
mixed with the sound of the stream.
Calista followed as fast as she could.

A little way up the creek was a log
bridge without a rail. Conrad had put
it up for his own convenience, and Calista never tried to cross it.

"Ach!" she thought, "I don't hope
she runs out there!" Then she began to
call, but Mary did not look back. She
fell over a root, picked herself up, and
went on, with her knees shaking.

Suddenly she began to cry very loud,
as a child does when it sees comfort, and
went on much faster, making for the
bridge. As she ran along the log her
arms were out to meet some one.

Calista stared for a couple of seconds,
then she raced like a savage down to the
first bend, her red shawl flying behind her.

It lay in a pool on the kitchen floor
when Conrad and Hannah came in; it
was the first thing they saw, and their
voices stopped as though a hand had been
laid upon their mouths. Mary was lying
on the settle and Calista was doubled up
against it with her face hidden.

"What's wrong?" Conrad asked. She
said nothing, and when he tried to lift
her she writhed away from him. Hannah
ran to Mary. The blankets were warm,
but the small creature was quite cold.

"Now it is time you say what has happened," she said, and Conrad stood silently by.

Calista sat up, looking deadly sick.
The story came out in fragments, and
at the end she bowed her head, shivering
and staring at nothing.

"Did she say this before?" Hannah
asked.

Calista told wearily, and the old woman listened, a spectator of strange things
to which she alone had the clue.

"Is that all?"

"Ach, yes! I can't remember any
more. Now do what you want to do."

Hannah spoke like a judge sentencing
a criminal: "So you thought she told lies
and you whipped her—that little thing!
Now I tell you something, Calista Yohe.

That night she was born I said to Mary—
your sister Mary!—that once she came on
Christmas she would be lucky and see
more than we see, and Mary was glad,
and the last thing she said was: 'I look
after her. I take care of her.' And they
say one that dies and leaves something
unfinished must come back to finish it
up. I guess Mary knew when to come.

"And you are glad. I don't say you
just wished this to her, but you thought
would be fine not to have her around
once you got married to Conrad. She
was lucky not to be here till you got a
good hold of her.

"You might have thought whether I
would let her with you that didn't want
her, to be in the way. But I am old.
It is a good thing Mary fetched her.
Now I see to her myself. Don't you dare
touch her."

Conrad had been perfectly still, with
the face of a man in a nightmare, but
now he went to the shaking woman and
lifted her in his arms. Hannah looked
at them for a moment. Then she set a
great kettle of water to heat, took up the
child and went out, leaving them alone
together, and they heard her footsteps
in the room above as she went back and
forth, getting what she needed.

The White Sleep of Auber Hurn

BY RICHARD RICE

THE thing happened in America; that is one reason for believing it. Another land would absorb it, or at least give a background to shadow over its likelihood, the scenery and atmosphere to lend an evanescent credibility, changing it in time to a mere legend, a tale told out of the hazy distance. But in America it obtrudes; it stares eternally on in all its stark unforgetfulness, absorbing its background, constantly rescuing itself from legend by turning guesswork and theory into facts, till it appears bare, irremediable, and complete,—witnessed at high noon, and in New Jersey of all places, flat, unillusive, and American.

The thing was as clear a fact in its unsubtle, shadowless mystery as was he—that is, as was the shell and husk of him lying there in the next room after I had watched the life and the person drawn out, leaving only mere barren lees to

show what had gone. Hours it lay there
to prove the thing, to settle it in my
mind, to let me believe eternally in it.
Then we buried it deep under the big
pile of scree on my hill. As I write I can
see the white stones from the window.

It is not all guesswork to begin with;
indeed it is not guesswork at any moment
if the end is always in view, and we had
to begin with the end. I tell you it was
as plain as daylight. People saw him,
heard him talk; saw him get off the train
at Newark to mail my letter—this one—
addressed to my engineers in Trenton;
heard him say, "Promised Crenshaw
to post this before reaching the city; guess
this is my last chance to keep it." It is
a little thing that counts; you can't get
by that; it alone is final; but there were a
dozen more. Ezekiel saw him on the
platform hunting for the right box for
west-bound mail, and saw him post the
letter after considerable trouble. When
I heard that, I yielded to the incredulous
so far as to telephone to Trenton, asking
if the firm had received it. I did that,
though I held the letter in my hand at
the time, and knew it had never left this
house. Ezekiel was sure that he mailed
the letter, that it went from his hand into
the box. He was watching carefully be-

cause just then the train began to move;
but Auber, leisurely ignoring this, appeared to be comparing his watch with the
station clock, and finally looked up at the
moving train as if in disapproval. Ezekiel lost sight of him in the crowd, and
then, at the same moment, he was taking
his seat opposite again.

Ezekiel said, "I thought you were
going to miss the train, characteristically,
for the sake of setting your watch." And
Auber replied, rather queerly: "Great
God! It's impossible now; I can see
that." Ezekiel did not know what he
meant, but remembered it afterward
when we were talking the whole thing
over in this room.

Besides Ezekiel, there were four men
who saw him after the train left Newark;
and the porter remembered holding the
vestibule door and trap-platform open for
some one as the train pulled out.

Then there is my coachman who drove
him to the train, here in Barrelton, who
had his tip of a silver dollar from him.
Put it in his pocket—and then—lost it,
of course. You see, there's the most conclusive link in the chain. If William had
produced his dollar, or my engineer had
received that letter, the whole thing
would fall through—jugglery and im-

position, mere ordinary faking. The
hypnotic theory might still hold, but it
must stretch fifty miles to an improbable
source in a man who is, at the time,
dying strangely on my bed.

Of course, there is no use asking if any
one on the train touched him,—not only
saw and heard him, but shook hands with
him, let us say. It is the same story as
William's, or not so good. Ezekiel is sure
that he shook hands when Auber first
boarded the train; Judson is sure that he
did so when he stepped across the aisle
to ask about me. Yet, I tell you that
would have made no difference; let him
have been as impalpable as the very air
of the car, those men would have felt the
flesh, just as William felt his silver dollar. "Fulfilment of sure expectation
on the ground of countless identical experiences," your psychologist would explain. Illusion and fact were indistin-
guishable; and though I happened to
watch the facts, and the others the illusion, their testimony is as good as mine.

There is the testimony of four men
that, when the smash came, they saw him
thrown from his seat, head first, into the
window-jamb, and lie for a moment half
through the shattered pane. Just before
this, he had taken out his watch. Its

3 S. H. D.

familiar picture-face, and also its enam-
elled hands exactly together at twelve
o'clock, had caught Ezekiel's eye. He
said that Auber looked at the watch, and
then leaned forward as if to call attention to the view from the window. It
was then that the smash came. When
Ezekiel and some others, who were only
thrown to the floor, looked up again,
Auber was gone.

You see, the time is identical; we cal-
culated it exactly, for the train left
Newark on time and takes just six minutes to reach the bridge; that is, at exactly noon. When I noticed the hour
here, it was, perhaps, a few minutes later,
and that is not a difference in time-
pieces, for it was by his own watch on
the bedside table. No one saw him on
the train or on the bridge after that. It
seems conclusive, just that alone. They
finally decided that he must have fallen
from the window and somehow rolled
from the sleepers into the river.

Actually no one else in the Pullman
was badly hurt. The men picked themselves up and rushed to the doors of the
car, or climbed out of the windows. Ezekiel put his head through the shattered
pane which Auber had struck. Men were
running toward the car ahead, from

which screams came. In the excitement
of rescuing those from the telescoped
coach, Auber was forgotten; but when it
was all over, Ezekiel and Judson looked
everywhere for him, till they assured
themselves that he was not on the bridge.

At all events, that is how he came to
be reported among "The Missing,—
known by friends to have been on the
train,—Auber Hurn, the artist."

During that night, when Ezekiel and
Judson had come down in response to my
telegrams, we sat here, talking endlessly,
guessing, relating, slowly developing the
theory of the thing, delving into our
minds for memories of him, gradually
getting below the facts, gradually working back to them, examining the connections, completing the chain. The main
fact, the culmination, had to be the soulless shell of him, lying there in the next
room. Our theory began far away from
that, in what he used to call "white
sleep," and more especially in a curious
occasional association between the dreams
of this sleep and the landscape pictures
that he painted. What impressed you
most as he recounted one of those half-
conscious dream concoctions, that he
named "white-sleep fancies," was the remarkable scenery, the setting of the

dream. This was in character with his
pictures, for about them both you felt
that peculiarly pervasive "sense of
place," for which his landscape is of
course famous, and which in these dreams
was emphasized through a subtle omi-
nousness of atmosphere. You perceived
what the place stood for, its sensational
elements, and you began vaguely to imagine the kind of event for which it
would form a suitable background. In
his pictures the element was a sort of
dream-infusion, as though in each scene
the secret goddess, the Naiad of the spot,
must have stood close to him as he painted, and thrilled him to understanding at
her impalpable touch. Whatever the
exact nature of these creative intuitions,
there was between his art and his dreams
a lurking connection, out of which, as we
believed, finally grew his strange faculty
for seeing beyond the scene, an intuition
for certain events associated with what
we called " an ominous locality."

This faculty began to distinguish itself
from mere psychical fancy through a
curious contact of one of Auber's dreams
with his actual experience.

The dream, which came at irregular intervals during a number of years, began
with a sense of color, a glare to dazzle

the eyes, till, as Auber insisted, he
awaked and saw the sunset glow over a
stretch of forest. He was on a hillside
field, spotted with daisies and clumps of
tall grass. On one side a stone wall, half
hidden by the grass and by a sumac
hedge in full bloom, curved over the sky-
line. All this was exactly expressible by
a gesture, and when he reached the bottom of the field he looked back for a long
time, and made the gesture apprecia-
tively. It was at this point that he always recognized the recurring dream;
but he could never remember how it was
going to end. Then he entered the wood
on a grassy path, and for a long time the
tall tasselled grasses brushed through his
fingers as he walked. Suddenly it grew
dark, and feeling that " it would be folly
to continue," he tried hard to remember
the point of the dream. Just as he seemed to recollect it, the sound of running
water came to him, as from a ravine, and
he knew that " he could not escape." The
low sound of running water,—the little
lonely gurgle of a deep-wood brook, all
but lost in the loam and brush of the silent
forest,—why should he feel an incomprehensible distaste for the place? He tried
feverishly to recollect the outcome of the
dream, but all memory of it had fled.

Nor could he bring himself to continue on the path; when he tried to take another step his leg dangled uselessly in front, his foot beating flimsily on the ground till he brought it back beside the other. The longer he listened to the sound of the running water, the stronger grew his aversion for the place. This continued indefinitely, till he awoke.

You perceived the vague sense of "ominous locality" developed out of the simplest details. There is a recognizable introduction, the field, the stone wall, the grass striking his fingers; but there is no ending, nothing happens; the dream-spell at last dissolves, and the sleeper wakes. His aversion to the sound of the brook can, therefore, come from no conscious knowledge of a portending catastrophe in the dream. It was always Auber's fancy that the dream would really end in a catastrophe, which, though the mind proper continue in ignorance, casts its ominous shadow through the sub-consciousness upon the surroundings of the event.

It was also a fanciful idea of his that dreams in general imply a subconscious state coexisting constantly with the actual realm of thought, but penetrated by our consciousness only when the will is

least active, or during sleep. With ordinary mortals sleep and consciousness are
so nearly incompatible that the notion of
actual mental achievement during sleep
is unthought of. Dreams are allowed to
run an absurd riot through the brain, dis-
turbing physical rest. The remedy for
this universal ailment and waste of time
was to be found in " white sleep," a bit of
Indian mysticism, purporting to accomplish a partial detachment of mind and
body, so that the will, which is always the
expression of the link between these two,
is, for the time, dissolved. The body
rests, but the unfettered mind enters
upon a " will-less state of pure seeing,"
where dreams no longer remain the meaningless fantasies of blind sleep, but become luminous with idea and sequence.
With the body thus left behind, the intel-
lect rises to the zenith of perception,
where the blue veil of earthly knowledge
is pierced and transcended.

How often had we heard Auber talk in
his fantastically learned fashion, with an
amused seriousness lighting up his face.
At what point he began to see something
more than amusement in his dreams and
theories, I never knew; but the serious
beginning of the thing took shape in an
incident which not even the most fervent

theorist could have created for the sake
of a theory.

It was up among the little knobby hills
to the north of my farm. We were as
usual sketching, and Auber had been
going on all the afternoon about the
mournful scenery, talking of nothing but
browns, and grays, and "mountain
melancholy." He had a way of stringing
out a ceaseless jargon while he worked,
—an irritating trick caught in the Paris
studios. At the end of the afternoon, he
held up a remarkable sketch, suggesting
the color scheme for a picture in the
atmosphere of oncoming dusk—a bit of
path over the hill toward the sun.

"You have struck it most certainly," I
said. "Be wary of finishing that; it is
strangely suggestive as it is."

He nodded; and then, as we packed up,
he said, "Do you know, I have felt
vaguely intimate with this spot, as if I
had been here before, as if I were paint-
ing a reminiscence." I remarked tritely
on the commonness of this feeling.

At the bottom of a hillside meadow I
was hunting for the entrance of a path
into a patch of woods. Auber, instead of
helping me, kept gazing back at the
fading light while he made random ob-
servations on the nature of the sky-line,

—one of his cant hobbies. "See how crudely the character of everything is defined up there against the sky," I heard him say, while I continued to search for the path. "Now even a sheep or a cow, or an inanimate thing, like that stone wall, for instance,—see how its character as a wall comes out as it sweeps over the top." At this moment, a little drop of surprise in his voice made me look around. He was walking backwards, one arm extended toward the hill in a descriptive gesture. "Why, it is the dream!" he murmured in hushed excitement. "Ah, of course! I might have known it. Now, I'll turn to find the path."

"I wish you would," I said.

He started abruptly. Then he came slowly, and touched me in a queer evasive way on my shoulder. Finally he drew a long breath, and gripped me by the arm. "Don't you recognize it?" "It's the dream! See! The stone wall—the field—the sumac! Now that's the first sumac—"

"Oh, come along!" I said; "there are twenty such fields. That is curious, though: you made the gesture. Do you recognize it all exactly?"

"It's it! the whole thing—and now, you see, I'm turning to find the path."

I admitted that it was curious, and
said that it would be interesting to see
how it all turned out.

For a long time Auber followed in
silence, which I tried to relieve by banter-
ing comments. I was some distance
ahead, when I heard him say, " The grass
is brushing through my hands."

" Why not?" I laughed, but it rang
false, for I recollected the detail. It was
childishly simple; perhaps that was why
the thing bothered me. I noticed that in
the growing darkness the forest took on a
peculiar look. It had been partly burnt
over, leaving the ground black, and some
of the trees gaunt, upbristling, and sen-
tinel-like. The place, even in broad daylight, would have had a night-struck appearance. At this hour, when the sudden
forest darkness had just fallen, there was
a sense of unusual gloom, easily connecting itself with strange forebodings.

Perhaps it had been five minutes, when
Auber said, " I am conscious that I cannot take my hands out of the grass."

As I said, it was a simple thing. With
an odd impulse, I groped back toward
him till I found his wrists, and then
shook them violently above his head.
We stood there for several moments performing this absurd pantomime in the

darkness. His arms, with the sleeves rolled up, felt heavy with flesh in my grip. I seemed to be handling things of dead, cold flesh.

Then Auber said, "I can still feel my hands down in the grass."

I drew back in a strange horror; but, at the same moment, we both stood stock-still to listen: from some distance to the right came the trickling sound of water. It was barely perceptible, and we listened hard, indefinitely, while the silence congealed in our ears, and the darkness condensed about our eyes, filling up space, and stopping thought save just for the sound of the brook. It seemed a sort of growing immobility, eternal, like after death.

At last Auber spoke, laying a hand on my shoulder: "It is over; let us go ahead."

After a while we talked about it. There was little to "go" on. You see, nothing happens, and, as Auber expressed it, "the psychological data are ineffective for lack of an event." But though the whole thing remained then a purely psychical experience, and did not "break through," yet it had something of the fulness of fate. Auber, as usual, had a theory: in the dream some manifestation was undoubtedly striving to break through, but he had been unable to facilitate the process. The present experience, he decided, was immature, a mere coincidence. The outcome might yet, however, be foreseen through the dream, if the creative perception of "white sleep" could be attained.

That is the affair which started the whole thing. Auber must have taken the suggestion it contained much more seriously than any of us for several years imagined; nor did we connect the long contemplativeness of the man with any definite purpose. The thing was too vague and illusive to become a purpose at all.

Before long there were half a dozen instances, some trivial, or seemingly coincidental, but all forming our theory. There is one Ezekiel recounted, as we sat here talking that night. It was just a matter of old Horace MacNair's coming in on them once during a thunder-storm. The family were sitting in the big hall; the ladies with their feet up on chairs to insulate them from the lightning; young Vincent Ezekiel teasing them by putting his on the mantelpiece. At one point in the storm came a terrible crash, and Auber jumped up, starting toward the door. Then he came back and sat down quietly, They laughed, and asked if he had been struck.

"No," he said, quite seriously, "not by the lightning, but by a curious idea that I saw Horace MacNair opening the door. I suppose I must have dreamed it; I was nearly asleep."

The Ezekiels looked at one another in surprise, and Mrs. Ezekiel said: "There is something curious in that, for the last time Horace was here, just before he died, he came in the midst of a thunder-storm as we were sitting here, much as we are now. And, why! I remember that he had come over because he expected to see you, but you had not arrived."

"That's so," put in young Vincent, "because he said that if you had been here, you wouldn't have been too afraid of the lightning to stand up and shake hands. And by Jove! I had my feet on the mantelpiece! I remember that, because when he saw me he laughed, and lined his up beside mine."

"He was wearing a gray rain-coat, and high overshoes that you made fun of," added Auber, shortly, and then kept an embarrassed silence.

That was true, Ezekiel said; and Auber had not seen the man in five years.

There were many cases which we
strung that night on the threads of our
theory, all working . toward its completion; and yet we neared the end with
misgiving and doubt, for we had the
necessity of believing, if we would keep
ourselves still sane. All of us had noticed
that so far as there was an element of
terror in the strange incidents, it lay
in the fact of a subtle undercurrent of
connections, as if Fate were dimly pointing all the while toward the invisible
culmination. Suddenly there would be
a new manifestation of Auber's faculty,
and a new instance would be added, illusive, baffling, and yet forming each time
new threads in the vague warp and woof
of something that we called our theory.
"There it is again," we would say to
ourselves, as we sent the ghostly shuttle
flying in our psychological loom.

This undercurrent appeared to touch
the incident of Horace MacNair, for it
seemed that the old artist had walked
over to the Ezekiels that night on purpose to talk with Auber about making
a series of pictures of the salt marshes
along the Passaic River. Old Horace
was dead of his heart before Auber arrived, but the suggestion was repeated
by Ezekiel; and Auber, taking it as some-

thing like a dying request from his old
master, besides appreciating its value, set
to work at once.

The long reaches of the Passaic tidal
lagoon, with their mists and blowing
swamp-grass, are crossed by the trestles
of all the railways which enter New York
from the south. It was old Horace Mac-
Nair's idea that this place, more travelled,
more unnoticed, and yet more picturesque,
perhaps, than any spot near the metrop-
olis, might be the making of Auber's
reputation. The varied, moody tones of
the marsh-land, forever blending in a
pervasive atmosphere of desolate beauty,
suited Auber's peculiar style. Here he
would paint what passed in the pop-
ular eye for the dullest commonplace,
and would interpret, at the same time,
both this landscape and his little-under-
stood art.

While he worked I frequently visited
Auber on his yawl *Houri,* which was can-
vassed over for an outdoor studio, and
anchored at the point from which he
wished to paint. One day we were tied
up to a pile by the Central Railroad
trestle. It was just the heat of the day,
and Auber, stretched out on a deck chair,
was taking a sort of siesta. His eyes
were closed, and he had let his cigar go

out. Whether it was due to the light through the colored awning, I was not sure, but I was suddenly attracted by a dull vacancy that seemed to be forming in his countenance. It stole upon the features as if they were being slowly sprinkled with fine dust, blotting their expression into a flat lifelessness. Then the rush of a train passing over the bridge disturbed him. With a fleeting look of pain he sat up, glanced first furtively at me, and then stared hard around.

"Was there a train?" he asked, at length.

"Yes—an express."

"It did not stop here on the bridge for anything?"

"No, of course not."

"Of course not," he agreed, absently. "How long ago?"

"Perhaps two minutes," I said.

He examined his watch. After a while he got up, seeming to pull himself together with an effort, and began scraping nervously on his picture. I noticed that the palette-knife trembled in his hand.

"What is the matter?" I asked, finally.

"I feel very much upset," he replied, and sank weakly on the hatch. "I was on that train and—"

I had to jump below to the ice-chest;

Auber seemed to have fainted. Jerry, the skipper, and I applied cold water for five minutes, and then Auber revived and asked for whiskey.

"I was on the train," he began again, persistently. "Several people, whom I knew, must have been in the chair-car with me, because I seemed to be taking part in a conversation. Was there a Pullman on the train?" he asked, abruptly.

"Yes," I said; "at the end."

The answer seemed to reassure him unhappily. "I was on the train," he continued, "but I could not think where I had come from. There were vague recollections of a walk, then of a long drive in the dark. Now I was on the train, and yet I was somehow not there even now." I poured out more whiskey, but he pushed it aside absently. "I was not there, nor was I here; for when I moved, something seemed to be folded about me, like bedclothes. It was all a kind of duplication, and I could be on the train or in the other place at will. That is why it seemed confused and unreal. We were talking about some matter of business. I held a list of figures that I referred to now and then. Once I leaned forward to look out of the window; it was just here. I was pointing, and saying to some one,

4   S. H. D.

'There is my last salt marsh!' when a
great shock stopped the words, and sent
me against something in front. For a moment I was conscious that you were leaning over me. Then I had a strange feeling of becoming gradually detached, as
if from my very self. A weight and a
feeling of bedclothes slipped from me;
there was alternate glaring light and
enveloping darkness. Finally the light
prevailed, and I found myself looking up
into this hideous awning."

"Well," I said, "that is a very queer
dream!"

"Yes; it was white sleep," he replied,
slowly; "but something was added this
time." He put his hand on my arm
appealingly. "I knew it would come;
I have had the beginnings of that dream
before." He spoke as if from a tragic
winding-sheet, a veil spun in the warp of
his own fancy and also in the very woof
of Fate; and out of this veil, through
which none of us ever saw, he was stretching his hand to ask of me—what?

I did what I could. Auber consented
to come at once to my farm till rest
should partly restore him. We reached
here that night. It was just two weeks
ago; in thought, it is, for me, a lifetime.
It was a time of suspense and wait-

ing when diversion seemed almost ir-
reverent, but at last it was forced upon
us by that ever-moving providence which
stood back of the whole affair. My dam
broke at the upper farm. Chance?
Nothing of the sort! I went up to see
how it had happened, and found some
rotten joists and rust-eaten girders. They
are in the course of events. Auber went
with me while I should see things set
to rights.

It was a simple incident, but somehow
I suspected it of finality even as we started out of the yard on the long drive. I
was suspicious of that knobby hill region,
which was connected with the incipient
indications of the whole affair. On ar-
riving in the late afternoon, however,
nothing could be more natural than that
Auber, having inspected the dam, should
stroll on to the pasture, where he once
sketched the path that runs down to his
dream-meadow.

I went back to the farmhouse, and
wrote to my engineers a detail of the
breach in the dam, then sat down on the
porch to enjoy a smoke. The day was
warm and dreamy; the sun, filtering
through the September haze, rested on the
eyelids like a caressing hand. I was soon
half asleep, peering lazily at the view

which zigzags down between the knobby
hills to the more cultivated farm-lands
that we had left hours behind us, when
the telephone rang. I got up and answered it:

"William?—at the farm? Oh yes—a
message, a telegram—for Mr. Hurn, you
say? Is it important?—Well, go ahead—
What! Must take 11.10 express—cri-
sis on Wall Street?—meet on train—
Who?—Ezekiel."

It had come, then! Chance? No. A
railroad merger; stockholders interested.
At first I said: "I won't tell him." Then
I thought: "After this supposed Sentence
is delayed and delayed till he no longer
looks on the world as his prison cell,
and the whole matter evaporates in a
psychological mist, he will say: 'Our
superstitions, my dear friend, and your
loving care, cost me just twenty thousand
dollars that trip. My picture of the twilight path, which you would have in-
terrupted, won't replace a hundredth part
of that.'"

I wandered down to the broken dam;
there beside the breach, with the river
sucking darkly through, Josiah Peacock
stood, contemplating the scene with his
practical eye against to-morrow's labor.
Suddenly I found myself mentioning the

telegram. He said, "Then you'll have
to drive back to-night." I felt alarmed;
surely this was none of my doing. Presently I was taking the short cut through
the woods. The red glow of sunset was
fading behind me, and darkness already gathered among the trees. Aware
of a vague anxiety that impelled me forward, an odd notion that I might be late
for something, I began to hurry along,
the gaunt tree trunks watching like sen-
tinels as I passed. Was I looking for
Auber Hurn? It was strangely remi-
niscent, not a real experience. "This is
absurd," I said to myself at length, and
straightened my foot to stop. Instead,
I unexpectedly leaped over a fallen
log, and continued with nervous strides,
while I flung back a sneaking glance
of embarrassment.

On the turns of the path darkness
closed in rapidly; the outlines of objects
loomed uncertainly distant through the
forest. Gradually I became aware that
at the end of a dim vista down which
I was hurrying, something white had
formed itself in the path. I stopped to
look, but could make out nothing clearly.
It remained dimly ahead, and I approached, a few steps at a time, peering
through the obscure gray shadows, stri-

ving to concentrate my vision. At last I recognized that it was Auber Hurn in his shirt-sleeves, standing still in the middle of the path. Apparently he, too, was trying to see who was coming.

"Auber!" I called. I was not sure that he replied.

When I was very close I began at once, as if involuntarily: "Auber, you see, I came to meet you. There is a message from Ezekiel—a Wall Street panic, or something. He wants you to meet him on the 11.10 to - mor— It will be necess— Auber?" Had I been talking to the air? I looked about me. "Auber! —Auber Hurn!" I called. There was no one there; but in the hush of listening there came, as if wandering to me through the forest, the little lost gurgle of a distant brook.

For a moment I stood fascinated by a reminiscence—and then, a sudden fear swelling in my throat, I ran. Back on the path I fled, my legs seeming to go of themselves, hurling my body violently along; my feet pounding behind, as if in pursuit, whirling around the turns, then down the last straight aisle, past the sentinel trees, out into the light.

When I reached the farmyard, a fresh team was being hitched to our carriage.

"What! Has Mr. Hurn come back?"
I asked, shakily.

"No," said Josiah, "but I thought
maybe you'd want things ready. Didn't
you find him?"

"Why—no," I replied, and then repeated firmly, "No, I did not."

I sat down, exhausted, on the porch,
and waited. At the end of ten minutes
Auber Hurn entered the gate, crossed to
the buggy, and got in. Josiah, from
between the horses where he was buck-
ling a knee-guard, looked up in surprise.
"You got that message, Mr. Hurn?"

"Yes," said Auber, speaking very distinctly. "Mr. Crenshaw just gave it
to me."

Josiah turned to me. "I thought you
said—" he began.

"I was mistaken—I mean, I misunder-
stood you," I interposed.

Josiah stared, and then finished the
harnessing. "Your coats are here under
the seat," he remarked. I took my place
mechanically. Mrs. Josiah came with
some milk and sandwiches. I finished
mine hurriedly, and took the reins.

Auber sank back into his corner without a word, leaving me to feel only a
sense of desperate confused isolation, of
lonely helplessness.

At length Auber said, in a voice that startled me, a low, contented voice: "You were on the path? You went to find me yourself?"

"Yes," I answered; and then, after a long time, "And you were not there—yourself?"

"No, I was not there." He leaned back against the cushions, and I thought he smiled. "I was in that hill meadow. I went to sleep there for a short time."

It was two o'clock when we drove into the yard. William was waiting to take the horses.

As we went into the house, William asked if he should have the trap for the 11.10 express. I could not answer, and Auber said, looking at me in the light of the open door, "Yes, certainly."

I can see him now in the cheerless white hallway, his tall figure exaggerated in a long driving-cloak, his high features sharpened in the light of the lantern.

In taking off my coat I felt, in the pocket, the letter I had written to my engineer in Trenton. I laid it on the hall table. "You might post that to-morrow before you get to New York," I said, casually.

Then I lighted him to his room, and we said "good night."

Undressing mechanically, I went to bed, and after a long time I slept, exhausted.

A rumbling noise; then, after it had ceased, the realization that a carriage had driven out of the yard—that was what woke me up. The clock on my bureau said half past ten. For a moment I forgot what that meant; and then sliding out of bed, I tiptoed quickly down the hall. Putting my ear to Auber's door, I listened—till I had made sure. From within came the dull breathing of a sleeper. Throwing on a few clothes, I went down-stairs. The waitress was dusting in the hall.

"Where has the carriage gone?" I asked her.

"Why, sir," she said, "William is taking Mr. Hurn to the station."

After a while I had the courage to say cautiously, "I thought Mr. Hurn was still asleep; I did not hear him come down."

"He came down ten minutes ago," she replied, "and in a great hurry, with no time for breakfast."

"You saw him?" I cross-examined.

"Yes. The carriage was waiting, and he seemed in a great hurry, though he did run back to take a letter from the table there."

I was standing between the table and
the maid.

"Well, of course you're right," I said,
carelessly, and at that moment I put my
hand on the letter. I turned my back
and put it in my pocket.

I went hurriedly to the barn. The run-
about trap and the mare were out. Then
I finished dressing, and had breakfast.
Soon after, William drove into the yard,
and I called from the library window—
"Where have you been?"

"Just to the station, sir."

"What for? Has my freight arrived?"

"Mr. Hurn, for the 11.10,"—he explained respectfully.

"Ah, yes!" I cried, in an overvoice;
"I keep forgetting that I have just waked
up. You saw him off? Ah—did he leave
any message for me? I overslept, and
did not see him this morning."

"No, sir; I had no message," he replied. "But he's a liberal man, Mr.
Hurn, sir." He grinned and slapped his
pocket; then, with a look of doubt, he
straightened out one leg to allow his
hand inside; the look grew more doubt-
ing; he stood up and searched system-
atically, under the seat, everywhere.

"Guess it rolled out," I said, very
much interested. "What was it?"

"A silver dollar," he answered, mournfully.

"Oh, well, I'll make that up," I called, and shut the window.

I took out my watch and made a calculation; Auber's train was probably at Newark. I could stand it no longer, and I went toward his room, stamping on the bare floor, whistling nervously, and rattling the rickety balustrade. I banged open the door and began to shout: "Auber! you've missed your—"

He did not move. He was lying on his back, with his arms extended evenly outside the bedclothes, which were tucked close around his breast. He lay as if in state, with that dull dusty pallor on his face, and that eyeless vacancy of an effigy on a marble tomb—a voidness of expression, with masklike indications of duration and immobility. On the reading-table, at his bedside, I noticed his watch lying face up. It was two or three minutes of the noon hour.

· Sitting down on the bed, I touched Auber on the shoulder. He did not move. An intuition, growing till it all but became an idea, and then remaining short of expressibility, unable to perceive even its own indefiniteness—a film for impressions where there is no light—such was the vagueness of my guess concerning the metamorphosis that was taking place. Yet I began to understand that Auber Hurn, the real man, was not there, not on the bed, not in my house at all. It was as if the Person were being gradually deducted, leaving only the prime flesh to vouch for the man's existence. Even as I sat in wonder, with my eyes upon him, the life tinge faded utterly from his skin. There was a fleeting shadow as if of pain. His breast sank in a long outbreathing, and then, after seconds and minutes, it did not rise again. I listened. The room seemed to be listening with me. The silence became stricken with awe, with the interminable and unanswering awe—the muteness of death.

We believed in the thing. Ezekiel and Judson came down in response to my telegrams, and we sat here talking it all over, hours through the night. It was inevitable to believe in it. We took his body up in the darkness, and buried it in the scree on my hill; then we came back to Auber's room, and faced each other by the empty bed.

"This is not for the practical world, or for the law," I said. "No coroner on earth could return a verdict here."

"We could never see the thing clearly again if the practical world got hold of it," said Judson. "Look; you have to believe so much!" He had picked up Auber's purse from the table, where it had lain beside his watch. He opened it over the bed. A roll of bills fell out—and one silver dollar.

"That belongs to William, before the law," said Ezekiel.

In Tenebras

A Parable

BY HOWARD PYLE

*O*NE *morning, after I had dressed myself and had left my room, I came upon an entry which I had never before noticed, even in this my own house. At the further end a door stood ajar, and wondering what was in the room beyond, I traversed the long passageway and looked within. There I saw a man sitting, with an open book lying upon his knees, who, as I laid one hand upon the door and opened it a little wider, beckoned to me to come and read what was written therein.*

A secret fear stirred and rustled in my heart, but I did not dare to disobey. So, coming forward (gathering away my clothes lest they should touch his clothes), I leaned forward and read these words:

"WHAT SHALL A MAN DO THAT HE MAY GAIN THE KINGDOM OF HEAVEN?"

*I did not need a moment to seek for
an answer to the question. " That," said
I, " is not difficult to tell,,for it has been
answered again and again. He who
would gain the kingdom of heaven must
resist and subdue the lusts of his heart;
he must do good works to his neighbors;
he must fear his God. What more is
there that man can do?"*

*Then the leaf was turned, and I read
the Parable.*

I.

The town of East Haven is the full
equation of the American ideal worked
out to a complete and finished result.
Therein is to be found all that is best
of New England intellectuality — well
taught, well trained; all that is best of
solidly established New England prosperity; all that is best of New England pro-
gressive radicalism, tempered, toned, and
governed by all that is best of New England conservatism, warmed to life by all
that is best and broadest of New England
Christian liberalism. It is the sum total of nineteenth-century American *cul-
tus,* and in it is embodied all that for
which we of these days of New World
life are striving so hard. Its municipal

government is a perfect model of a municipal government; its officials are elected from the most worthy of its prosperous middle class by voters every one of whom can not only read the Constitution, but could, if it were required, analyze its laws and by-laws. Its taxes are fairly and justly assessed, and are spent with a well-considered and munificent liberality. Its public works are the very best that can be compassed, both from an artistic and practical stand-point. It has a free library, not cumbersomely large, but almost perfect of its kind; and, finally, it is the boast of the community that there is not a single poor man living within its municipal limits.

Its leisure class is well read and widely speculative, and its busy class, instead of being jealous of what the other has attained, receives gladly all the good that it has to impart.

All this ripeness of prosperity is not a matter of quick growth of a recent date; neither is its wealth inherited and held by a few lucky families. It was fairly earned in the heyday of New England commercial activity that obtained some twenty-five or thirty years ago, at which time it was the boast of East Haven people that East Haven sailing-vessels

covered the seas from India to India.
Now that busy harvest-time is passed and
gone, and East Haven rests with opulent
ease, subsisting upon the well-earned
fruits of good work well done.

With all this fulness of completion one
might think that East Haven had attained
the perfection of its ideal. But no. Still
in one respect it is like the rest of the
world; still, like the rest of the world,
it is attainted by one great nameless sin,
of which it, in part and parcel, is somehow guilty, and from the contamination
of which even it, with all its perfection
of law and government, is not free. Its
boast that there are no poor within its
limits is true only in a certain particular
sense. There are, indeed, no poor resi-
dent, tax-paying, voting citizens, but during certain seasons of the year there
are, or were, plenty of tramps, and they
were not accounted when that boast was
made.

East Haven has clad herself in comely
enough fashion with all those fine garments of enlightened self - government,
but underneath those garments are, or
were, the same vermin that infested the
garments of so many communities less
clean—parasites that suck existence from
God's gifts to decent people. Indeed,

that human vermin at one time infested
East Haven even more than the other
and neighboring towns; perhaps just because its clothing of civilization was
more soft and warm than theirs; perhaps
(and upon the face this latter is the more
likely explanation of the two) because,
in a very exaltation of enlightenment,
there were no laws against vagrancy.
Anyhow, however one might account for
their presence, there the tramps were.
One saw the shabby, homeless waifs
everywhere—in the highways, in the byways. You saw them slouching past the
shady little common, with its smooth
greensward, where well - dressed young
ladies and gentlemen played at lawn-
tennis; you saw them standing knocking
at the doors of the fine old houses in Bay
Street to beg for food to eat; you saw
them in the early morning on the steps
of the old North Church, combing their
shaggy hair and beards with their fingers,
after their night's sleep on the old
colonial gravestones under the rustling
elms; everywhere you saw them—heavy,
sullen-browed, brutish—a living reproach
to the well - ordered, God - fearing community of something cruelly wrong,
something bitterly unjust, of which they,
as well as the rest of the world, were

guilty, and of which God alone knew the remedy.

No town in the State suffered so much from their infestation, and it was a common saying in the town of Norwark—a prosperous manufacturing community adjoining East Haven—that Dives lived in East Haven, and that Lazarus was his most frequent visitor.

The East Haven people always felt the sting of the suggested sneer; but what could they do? The poor were at their doors; they knew no immediate remedy for that poverty; and they were too compassionate and too enlightened to send the tramps away hungry and forlorn.

So Lazarus continued to come, and Dives continued to feed him at the gate, until, by-and-by, a strange and unexpected remedy for the trouble was discovered, and East Haven at last overcame its dirty son of Anak.

II.

Perhaps if all the votes of those ultra-intelligent electors had been polled as to which one man in all the town had done most to insure its position in the van of American progress; as to who best repre-

sented the community in the matter of
liberal intelligence and ripe culture; as
to who was most to be honored for stead-
fast rectitude and immaculate purity of
life; as to who was its highest type of enlightened Christianity—an overwhelming
if not unanimous vote would have been
cast for Colonel Edward Singelsby.

He was born of one of the oldest and
best New England families; he had grad-
uated with the highest honors from Har-
vard, and finished his education at Göt-
tingen. At the outbreak of the rebellion
he had left a lucrative law practice and a
probable judgeship to fight at the head
of a volunteer regiment throughout the
whole war, which he did with signal
credit to himself, the community, and the
nation at large. He was a broad and profound speculative thinker, and the papers
which he occasionally wrote, and which
appeared now and then in the more
prominent magazines, never failed to attract general and wide-spread attention.
His intelligence, clear-cut and vividly
operating, instead of leading him into
the quicksands of scepticism, had never
left the hard rock of earnest religious belief inherited from ten generations of
Puritan ancestors. Nevertheless, though
his feet never strayed from that rock, his

was too active and living a soul to rest
content with the arid face of a by-gone
orthodoxy; God's rain of truth had fallen
upon him and it, and he had hewn and
delved until the face of his rock blos-
somed a very Eden of exalted Christianity. To sum up briefly and in full,
he was a Christian gentleman of the
highest and most perfect type.

Besides his close and profound studies
in municipal government, from which
largely had sprung such a flawless and
perfect type as that of East Haven, he
was also interested in public charities,
and the existence of many of the bene-
ficial organizations throughout the State
had been largely due to his persistent
and untiring efforts. The municipal re-
forms, as has been suggested, worked
beautifully, perfectly, without the grating of a wheel or the creaking of a joint;
but the public charities—somehow they
did not work so well; they never did just
what was intended, or achieved just
what was expected; their mechanism appeared to be perfect, but, as is so univer-
sally the case with public charities, they
somehow lacked a soul.

It was in connection with the matter of
public charities that the tramp question
arose. Colonel Singelsby grappled with

it, as he had grappled with so many matters of the kind. The solution was the
crowning work of his life, and the result
was in a way as successful as it was para-
doxical and unexpected.

Connected with the East Haven Public
Library was the lecture-room, where an
association, calling itself the East Haven
Lyceum, and comprising in its number
some of the most advanced thinkers of
the town, met on Thursdays from November to May to discuss and digest matters social and intellectual. More than
one good thing that had afterward taken
definite shape had originated in the dis-
cussions of the Lyceum, and one winter,
under Colonel Singelsby's lead, the tramp
question was taken up and dissected.

He had, Colonel Singelsby said, studied
that complex question very earnestly and
for some time, and to his mind it had re-
solved itself to this: not how to suppress
vagrancy, but how to make of the vagrant
an honest and useful citizen. Repressive
laws were easily passed, but it appeared
to him that the only result achieved by
them was to drive the tramp into other
sections where no such laws existed, and
which sections they only infested to a
greater degree and in larger numbers.
Nor in these days of light was it, in his

opinion, a sufficient answer to that objection that it was the fault of those other communities that they did not also pass repressive laws. The fact remained that they had not passed them, and that the tramps did infest their precincts, and such being the case, it was as clear as day (for that which injures some, injures all) that the wrong of vagrancy was not corrected by merely driving tramps over the limits of one town into those of another. Moreover, there was a deeper and more interior reason against the passage of such repressive laws; to his thinking it behooved society, if it would root out this evil, to seek first the radix from which it drew existence; it behooved them first to very thoroughly diagnose the disease before attempting a hasty cure. "So let us now," said he, "set about searching for this radix, and then so drive the spade of reform as to remove it forever."

The discussion that followed opened a wide field for investigation, and the conclusion finally reached during the winter was not unlike that so logically deduced by Mr. Henry George at a later date. The East Haven Lyceum, however, either did not think of or did not care to advocate such a radical remedy as

Mr. George proposes. They saw clearly
enough that, apart from the unequal dis-
tribution of wealth, which may perhaps
have been the prime cause of the trouble,
idleness and thriftlessness are acquired
habits, just as industry and thrift are acquired habits, and it seemed to them better to cure the ill habit rather than to
upset society and then to rebuild it again
for the sake of benefiting the ill-con-
ditioned few.

So the result of the winter's talk was
the founding of the East Haven Refuge,
of which much has since been written
and said.

Those interested in such matters may
perhaps remember the article upon the
Refuge published in one of the prominent
magazines. A full description of it was
given in that paper. The building stood
upon Bay Street overlooking the harbor;
it was one of the most beautiful situa-
tions in the town; without, the building
was architecturally plain, but in perfect
taste; within, it was furnished with every
comfort and convenience—a dormitory
immaculately clean; a dining-room, large
and airy, where plain substantial food,
cooked in the best possible manner, was
served to the inmates. There were three
bath-rooms supplied with hot and cold

water, and there was a reading and a
smoking-room provided not only with all
the current periodicals, but with chess,
checkers, and backgammon-boards.

At the same time that the Refuge was
being founded and built, certain municipal laws were enacted, according to
which a tramp appearing within the
town limits was conveyed (with as little
appearance of constraint as possible) to
the Refuge. There for four weeks he was
well fed, well clothed, well cared for.
In return he was expected to work for
eight hours every day upon some piece
of public improvement: the repaving of
Main Street with asphaltum blocks was
selected by the authorities as the initial
work. At the end of four weeks the
tramp was dismissed from the Refuge
clad in a neat, substantial, well-made suit
of clothes, and with money in his pocket
to convey him to some place where he
might, if he chose, procure permanent
work.

The Refuge was finished by the last of
March, and Colonel Singelsby was unani-
mously chosen by the board as superintendent, a position he accepted very reluctantly. He felt that in so accepting
he shouldered the whole responsibility of
the experiment that was being under-

taken, yet he could not but acknowledge
that it was right for him to shoulder that
burden, who had been foremost both in
formulating and advocating the scheme,
as well as most instrumental in carrying
it to a practical conclusion. So, as was
said, he accepted, though very reluctantly.

The world at large was much disposed
to laugh at and to ridicule all the prepa-
ration that Dives of East Haven made to
entertain his Lazarus. Nevertheless, there
were a few who believed very sincerely in
the efficacy of the scheme. But both
those who believed and those who scoffed
agreed in general upon one point—that it
was altogether probable that East Haven
would soon be overrun with such a wilderness of tramps that fifty Refuges would
not be able to supply them with refuge.

But who shall undertake to solve that
inscrutable paradox, human life — its
loves, its hates?

The Refuge was opened upon the 1st of
April; by the 29th there were thirty-two
tramps lodged in its sheltering arms, all
working their eight hours a day upon the
repaving of Main Street. That same day
—the 29th — five were dismissed from
within its walls. Colonel Singelsby, as
superintendent, had a little office on the
ground-floor of the main building, open-

ing out upon the street. At one o'clock, and just after the Refuge dinner had been served, he stood beside his table with five sealed envelopes spread out side by side upon it. Presently the five outgoing guests slouched one by one into the room. Each was shaven and shorn; each wore clean linen; each was clad in a neat, plain, gray suit of tweed; each bore stamped upon his face a dogged, obstinate, stolid, low-browed shame. The colonel gave each the money enclosed in the envelope, thanked each for his service, inquired with pleasant friendliness as to his future movements and plans, invited each to come again to the Refuge if he chanced to be in those parts, shook each by a heavy, reluctant hand, and bade each a good-by. Then the five slouched out and away, leaving the town by back streets and byways; each with his hat pulled down over his brows; each ten thousand times more humiliated, ten thousand times more debased in his cleanliness, in his good clothes, and with money in his pocket, than he had been in his dirt, his tatters, his poverty.

They never came back to East Haven again.

The capacity of the Refuge was 50. In May there were 47 inmates, and Colonel

Singelsby began to apprehend the pre-
dicted overflow.   The overflow never
came. In June there were 45 inmates; in
July there were 27; in August there were
28; in September, 10; in October, 2; in
November, 1; in December there were
·none. The fall was very cold and wet,
and maybe that had something to do with
the sudden falling off of guests, for the
tramp is not fond of cold weather. But
even granting that bad weather had something to do with the matter, the Refuge
was nevertheless a phenomenal, an extraordinary success—but upon very different lines than Colonel Singelsby had
anticipated; for even in this the first
season of the institution the tramps began to shun East Haven even more sedu-
lously than they had before cultivated
its hospitality. Even West Hampstead,
where vagrancy was punished only less
severely than petty larceny, was not so
shunned as East Haven with the horrid
comforts of its Refuge.

III.

As was said, the records of the Refuge
showed that one inmate still lingered in
the sheltering arms of that institution

during a part of the month of November.
That one was Sandy Graff.

Sandy Graff did not strictly belong to
the great peregrinating leisure class for
whose benefit the Refuge had been more
especially founded and built. Those were
strangers to the town, and came and went
apparently without cause for coming and
going. Little or nothing was known of
such—of their name, of their life, of
whence they came or whither their footsteps led. But with Sandy Graff it was
different; he belonged identically to the
place, and all the town knew him, the
sinister tragedy of his history, and all the
why and wherefore that led to his becoming the poor miserable drunken outcast—
the town "bummer"—that he was.

There is something bitterly enough pathetic in the profound abasement of the
common tramp—frouzy, unkempt, dirty,
forlorn; without ambition further than
to fill his belly with the cold leavings
from decent folks' tables; without other
pride than to clothe his dirty body with
the cast-off rags and tatters of respectability; without further motive of life
than to roam hither and yon—idle, useless, homeless, aimless. In all this there
is indeed enough of the pathetic, but
Sandy Graff in his utter and complete

abasement was even more deeply, tragi-
cally sunken than they. For them there
was still some sheltering ægis of secrecy
to conceal some substratum in the utter-
most depths of personal depravity; but
for Sandy—all the world knew the story
of his life, his struggle, his fall; all the
world could see upon his blotched and
bloated face the outer sign of his inner
lusts; and what deeper humiliation can
there be than for all one's world to know
how brutish and obscene one may be in
the bottom of one's heart? What deeper
shame may any man suffer than to have
his neighbors read upon his blasted front
the stamp and seal of all, all his heart's
lust, set there not only as a warning and
a lesson, not only a visible proof how deep
below the level of savagery it is possible
for a God-enlightened man to sink, but
also for self-gratulation of those righteous ones that they are not fallen from
God's grace as that man has fallen?

One time East Haven had been Sandy
Graff's home, and it was now the centre
of his wanderings, which never extended
further than the immediately neighboring
towns. At times he would disappear
from East Haven for weeks, maybe
months; then suddenly he would appear
again, pottering aimlessly, harmlessly,

around the streets or byways; wretched,
foul, boozed, and sodden with vile rum,
which he had procured no one knew how
or where. Maybe at such times of re-
appearance he would be seen hanging
around some store or street corner,
maundering with some one who had
known him in the days of his prosperity,
or maybe he would be found loitering
around the kitchen or out-house of some
pitying Bay-Streeter, who also had known
him in the days of his dignity and cleanliness, waiting with helpless patience for
scraps of cold victuals or the dregs of the
coffee-pot, for no one drove him away or
treated him with unkindness.

Sandy Graff's father had been a cobbler
in Upper Main Street, and he himself had
in time followed the same trade in the
same little, old-fashioned, dingy, shingled,
hip-roofed house. In time he had married a good, sound-hearted, respectable
farmer's daughter from a neck of land
across the bay, known as Pig Island, and
had settled down to what promised to be
a decent, prosperous life.

So far as any one could see, looking
from the outside, his life offered all that
a reasonable man could ask for; but
suddenly, within a year after he was
married, his feet slipped from the beaten

level pathway of respectability. He began taking to drink.

Why it was that the foul fiend should
have leaped astride of his neck, no man
can exactly tell. More than likely it was
inheritance, for his grandfather, who had
been a ship-captain—some said a slave-
trader—had died of *mania a potu,* and it
is one of those inscrutable rulings of Di-
vine Providence that the innocent ones
of the third and fourth generation shall
suffer because of the sins of their fore-
bears, who have raised more than one
devil to grapple with them, their children, and children's children. Anyhow,
Sandy fell from grace, and within three
years' time had become a confirmed
drunkard.

Fortunately no children were born to
the couple. But it was one of the most
sad, pitiful sights in the world to see
Sandy's patient, sad-eyed wife leading
him home from the tavern, tottering, reeling, helpless, sodden. Pitiful indeed!
Pitiful even from the outside; but if one
could only have looked through that outer
husk of visible life, and have beheld the
inner workings of that lost soul—the
struggles, the wrestling with the foul
grinning devil that sat astride of him—
how much more would that have been

pitiful! And then, if one could have
seen and have realized as the roots from
which arose those inner workings, the
hopes, the longings for a better life that
filled his heart during the intervals of
sobriety, if one could have sensed but
one pang of that hell-thirst that foreran
the mortal struggle that followed, as that
again foreran the inevitable fall into his
kennel of lust, and then, last and greatest, if those righteous neighbors of his
who never sinned and never fell could
only have seen the wakening, the bitter
agony of remorse, the groaning horror of
self-abasement that ended the debauch-
ery— Ah! that, indeed, was something
to pity beyond man's power of pitying.

If Sandy's wife had only berated and
abused him, if she had even cried or made
a sign of her heart-break, maybe his
pangs of remorse might not have been so
deadly bitter and cruel; but her stead-
fast and unrelaxing patience—it was that
that damned him more than all else to
his hell of remorse.

At last came the end. One day Sandy
went to New Harbor City to buy leather
for cobbling, and there his devil, for no
apparent reason at all, leaped upon him
and flung him. For a week he saw or
knew nothing but a whirling vision of

the world seen through rum-crazy eyes;
then at last he awoke to find himself hat-
less, coatless, filthy, unshaved, blear-eyed,
palsied. Not a cent of money was left,
and so that day and night, in spite of the
deadly nausea that beset him and the
trembling weakness that hung like a
leaden weight upon every limb, he walked
all the thirty-eight miles home again to
East Haven. He reached there about
five o'clock, and in the still gray of the
early dawning. Only a few people were
stirring in the streets, and as he slunk
along close to the houses, those whom he
met turned and looked after him. No
one spoke to him or stopped him, as
might possibly have been done had he
come home at a later hour. Every shred
and filament of his poor remorseful heart
and soul longed for home and the comfort
that his wife alone could give him, and
yet at the last corner he stopped for a
quaking moment or so in the face of the
terror of her unreproachful patience.
Then he turned the corner—

Not a sign of his house was to be seen
—nothing but an empty, gaping blackness where it had stood before. *It had
been burned to the ground!*

Why is it that God's curse rests very
often and most heavily upon the misfor-

tunate? Why is it that He should crush
the reeds that are bruised beneath His
heel? Why is it that He should seem so
often to choose the broken heart to grind
to powder?

Sandy's wife had been burned to death
in the fire!

From that moment Sandy Graff was
lost, utterly and entirely lost. God, for
His terrible purposes, had taken away the
one last thread that bound the drowning
soul to anything of decency and cleanliness. Now his devil and he no longer
struggled together; they walked hand in
hand. He was without love, without
hope, without one iota that might bring a
flicker of light into the midnight gloom
of his despairing soul.

After the first dreadful blast of his sorrow and despair had burned itself out, he
disappeared, no one knew whither. A
little over a month passed, and then he
suddenly appeared again, drunken, maudlin, tearful. Again he disappeared, again
he reappeared, a little deeper sunken, a
little more abased, and henceforth that
was his life. He became a part of the
town, and everybody, from the oldest to
the youngest, knew him and his story.
He injured no one, he offended no one,
and he never failed, somehow or some-

where, to find food to eat, lodging for his
head, and clothing to cover his nakedness.
He had been among the very first to enter
the Refuge, and now, in November, he
was the last one left within its walls. He
was the only one of the guests who returned, and perhaps he would not have
done so had not his aching restlessness
driven him back to suffer an echo of
agony in the place where his damnation
had been inflicted upon him.

Between Colonel Singelsby upon the
one side, the wise, the pure, the honored
servant of God, and Sandy Graff upon
the other side, the vile, the filthy, the
ugly, the debased, there yawned a gulf
as immeasurably wide and deep as that
which gaps between heaven and hell.

IV.

The winter of the year that saw the
opening of the East Haven Refuge was
one of the most severe that New England
had known for generations. It was early
in January that there came the great
snowstorm that spread its two or three
feet of white covering all the way from
Maine to Virginia, and East Haven, looking directly in the teeth of the blast that

came swirling and raging across the open
harbor, felt the full force of the icy
tempest. The streets of the town lay a
silent desert of drifting whiteness, for
no one who could help it was abroad
from home that bitter morning.

The hail and snow spat venomously
against the windows of Dr. Hunt's office
in one of those fine old houses on Bay
Street overlooking the harbor. The wind
roared sonorously through the naked, tort-
ured branches of the great elm-trees, and
the snow piled sharp and smooth in fence
corners and around north gables of the
house.

Dr. Hunt shuddered as he looked out of
the window, for while all his neighbors
sat snug and warm around their hearths,
he had to face the raging of the icy blast
upon the dull routine of his business of
mercy—the dull routine of bread-getting
by comforting the afflictions of others.
Then the sleigh drew up to the gate, the
driver already powdered with the gathering whiteness, and Dr. Hunt struggled
into his overcoat, tied the ribbons of his
fur cap under his chin, and drew on his
beaver gloves. Then, with one final shud-
der, he opened his office door, and stepped
out into the drift upon the step.

Instantly he started back with a cry:

he had trodden upon a man covered and
hidden by the snow.

It was Sandy Graff. How long he had
been lying there, no one might tell; a
few moments more, and the last flicker of
life would have twinkled mercifully out.
The doctor had him out of the snow in a
moment, and in the next had satisfied
himself that Sandy was not dead.

Even as he leaned over the still white
figure, feeling the slow faint beating of
the failing heart, the doctor was consider-
ing whether he should take Sandy into
the house or not. The decision was almost instantaneous: it would be most in-
convenient, and the Refuge was only a
stone's-throw away. So the doctor did
not even disturb the household with the
news of what had happened. He and
the driver wrapped the unconscious figure in a buffalo-robe and laid it in the
sleigh.

As the doctor was about to step into
the sleigh, some one suddenly laid a heavy
hand upon his shoulder. He turned
sharply, for he had not heard the approaching footsteps, muffled by the thick
snow, and he had been too engrossed
with attention to Sandy Graff to notice
anything else.

It was young Harold Singelsby; his

face was very white and drawn, and in
the absorption of his own suppressed agitation he did not even look at Sandy.
"Doctor," said he, in a hoarse, constrained voice, "for God's sake, come home
with me as quickly as you can: father's
very sick!"

*I had often wondered how it is with
a man when he closes his life to this
world. Looking upon the struggling efforts of a dying man to retain his hold
upon his body, I had often wondered
whether his sliding to unconsciousness
was like the dissolving of the mind to
sleep in this life.*
*That death was not like sleep was at
such times patent enough—it was patent enough that it was the antithesis of
sleep. Sleep is peaceful; death is con-
vulsed—sleep is rest; death is separa-
tion.*
*That which I here following read in
the book as it lay open upon the man's
knees seemed in a way dark, broken, indistinct with a certain grim obscurity;
yet if I read truly therein I distinguished this great difference between death
and sleep: Sleep is the cessation of consciousness from an interior life to exterior thought; death is the cessation of*

*consciousness from the exterior mind to
an interior life.*

When Sandy Graff opened his eyes
once more, it was to find himself again
within the sheltering arms of the Refuge.
That awakening was almost to a full and
clear consciousness. It was with no confusion of thought and but little confusion
of sight, except .for a white mist that
seemed to blur the things he saw.

He knew, instantly and vividly, where
he was.   Instantly and vividly everything found its fit place in his mind—the
long rows of cots; the bald, garishly white
walls, cold and unbeautiful in their immaculate cleanliness; the range of curtainless windows looking out upon the
chill, thin gray of the winter day. He
was not surprised to find himself in
the Refuge; it did not seem strange to
him, and he did not wonder. He dimly
remembered stumbling through the snow-
drifts and then falling asleep, overpowered by an irresistible and leaden drowsiness. But just where it was he fell, he
could not recall.

He saw with dim sight that three or
four people were gathered about his bed.
Two of them were rubbing his legs and
feet, but he could not feel them. It was

this senselessness of feeling tha(first
brought the jarring of the truth to him.
The house-steward stood near by, and
Sandy turned his face weakly toward
him. "Mr. Jackson," said he, faintly,
"I think I'm going to die."

He turned his face again (now toward
the opened window), and was staring un-
winkingly at a white square of light, and
it seemed to him to grow darker and darker. At first he thought that it was the
gathering of night, but faint and flickering as were his senses, there was something beneath his outer self that dreaded
it—that dreaded beyond measure the
coming of that darkness. After one or
two efforts, in which his stiff tongue re-
fused to form the words he desired to
speak, he said, at last, "I can't see; it's
—getting—dark."

He was dimly, darkly conscious of hurry and bustle around him, of voices calling to send for the doctor, of hurrying
hither and thither, but it all seemed faint
and distant. Everything was now dark
to his sight, and it was as though all this
concerned another; but as outer things
slipped further and further from him, the
more that inner life struggled, tenacious-

ly, dumbly, hopelessly, to retain its grip
upon the outer world. Sometimes, now
and then, to this inner consciousness, it
seemed almost as though it were rising
again out of the gathering blackness.
But it was only the recurrent vibrations
of ebbing powers, for still again, and
even before it knew it, that life found
itself quickly deeper and more hopelessly
in the tremendous shadow into which it
was being inexorably engulfed.

He himself knew nothing now of those
who stood about the bed, awe-struck and
silent, looking down upon him; he himself sensed nothing of the harsh convul-
sive breathing, and of all the other grim
outer signs of the struggle. But still,
deep within, that combat of resistance to
death waged as desperately, as vividly, as
ever.

A door opened, and at the sudden noise
the dissolving life recrystallized for one
brief instant, and in that instant the dying man knew that Dr. Hunt was standing beside his bed, and heard him say, in
a slow, solemn voice, sounding muffled
and hollow, as though from far away and
through an empty space, "Colonel Singelsby has just died."

Then the cord, momentarily drawn

tense, was relaxed with a snap, and the last smoky spark was quenched in blackness.

Dr. Hunt's fingers were resting lightly upon the wrist. As the last deep quivering breath expired with a quavering sigh, he laid the limp hand back upon the bed, and then, before he arose, gently closed the stiff eyelids over the staring glassy eyes, and set the gaping jaws back again into a more seemly repose.

V.

So all this first part of the Parable had, as I read it, a reflected image of what was real and actual; of what belonged to the world of men as I knew that world. The people of whom it spoke moved and lived, maybe not altogether as real men of flesh and blood move and live, but nevertheless with a certain life of their own—images of what was real. All these things, I say (excepting perhaps the last), were clear and plain enough after a certain fashion, but that which followed showed those two of whom the story was written— the good man and the wicked man— stripped of all their outer husk of fleshly reality, and walking and talking not

*as men of flesh and blood, but as men in
the spirit.*

*So, though I knew that which I was
reading might indeed be as true, and
perhaps truer, than that other which I
had read, and though I knew that to such
a state I myself must come, and that as
these two suffered, I myself must some
time suffer in the same kind, if not in
the same degree, nevertheless it was all
strangely unreal, and being set apart
from that which I knew, was like life as
seen in a dream.*

*Yet let it not be thought that this Par-
able is all a vague dream, for there are
things which are more real than reality,
and being so, must be couched in different words from such as describe the
things that one's bodily eyes behold of the
grim reality of this world. Such things,
being so told, may seem as strange and
as unsubstantial as that which is unreal,
instead of like that which is real.*

*So that which is now to be read must
be read as the other has been read—not
as a likeness of life in its inner being,
but as an image of that life.*

Sandy Graff awoke, and opened his
eyes. At first he thought that he was
still within the dormitory of the Refuge,

for there before him he saw cold, bare
white walls immaculately clean. Upon
either hand was the row of beds, each
with its spotless coverlet, and in front
was the long line of curtainless windows
looking out upon the bright daylight.

But as his waking senses gathered to a
more orderly clearness, he saw very soon
that the place in which he was was very
different from the Refuge. Even newly
awakened, and with his brain clouded and
obscured by the fumes of sleep, he distinguished at once that the strange, clear,
lucid brilliancy of the light which came
in through the row of windows was very
different from any light that his eyes had
ever before seen. Then, as his mind
opened wider and fuller and clearer, and
as one by one the objects which surrounded him began to take their proper place in
his awakened life, he saw that there were
many people around, and that most of the
beds were occupied, and in every case by
a man. The room in which he lay was
somewhat longer than the dormitory of
the Refuge, and was connected at the further end with what appeared to be a sort
of waiting-room beyond. In and out of
the connecting doorway people were coming and going. Some of these seemed
to be friends of those who were lying in

the beds, being in every case led to some
particular bedside, the occupant of which
had newly awakened; others, who seemed
to be attendants of the place, moved constantly hither and thither, busying themselves around other of the beds, where lay
such as seemed to need attention.

Sandy looked slowly around him from
left to right. Some of the occupants of
the beds—and one of these lay in the cot
next to him—were not yet awake, and he
saw, with a sort of awe, that each of these
lay strangely like a dead man—still, motionless, the face covered with a linen
napkin. Two of the attendants seemed
to have these sleepers especially in their
charge, moving continually hither and
thither, to the bedside first of one and
then another, evidently to see if there
were yet any signs of waking. As Sandy
continued watching them, he saw them
at last softly and carefully lift a napkin from one of the faces, whereupon
the man immediately awoke and sat up.

This occurred in a bed not very far
from where he himself lay, and he watched all that passed with a keen and
thrilling interest. The man had hardly
awakened when word was passed down
the length of the room to the antecham-
ber beyond. Apparently some friends of

the sleeper were waiting for this word
to be brought to them, for there entered
directly two women and a man from the
further doorway. The three came straight
to the bed in which the man lay, and
with great noise of rejoicing seemed to
welcome the new-comer. They helped
him to arise, handed him his clothes
piece by piece from the chair at the bedside, and the man began dressing himself.

It was not until then, and until his
ear caught some stray words of those
that were spoken, that Sandy began to
really realize where he was and what
had happened to him. Then suddenly a
great and awful light broke upon him
—he had died and had come to life again
—his living senses had solved the greatest of all mysteries—the final mystery;
the mystery of eternity.

It happens nearly always, it is said,
that the first awakening thought of those
who die is of the tremendous happening
that has . come upon them. So it was
with Sandy. For a while he lay quite
still, with his hands folded, and a strange
awful brooding, almost as though of fear,
breathlessly wrapping his heart roundabout. But it was not for a long time
that he lay thus, for suddenly, like a second flash of lightning in the gathering

darkness of a cloud, the thought shot
through him that no friends had come to
meet and to greet him as they had come
to meet and greet these others. Why had
his wife not come to him? He turned
his head; the chair beside him was
empty; he was without even clothes to
wear.

For a while he lay with closed eyes
like one stunned. Then a sudden voice
broke upon his ear, and he opened his
eyes again and looked up. A tall man
with calm face — almost a stern face—
stood beside the bed looking down at
him.

Somehow Sandy knew that he had no
business in the bed now that he was
awake, and, with a half-muttered apol-
ogy, he made a motion as if to arise,
then, remembering that there were no
clothes for him to wear, he sank back
again upon the pillow.

"Come," said the man, giving his cane
a rap upon the floor, "you must get up;
you have already been here longer than
the law allows."

Sandy had been too long accustomed
to self-abasement in the world he had
left to question the authority of the man
who spoke to him. "I can't help lying
here, sir," said he, helplessly. "I've no

clothes to wear." Then he added: "Maybe if you let my wife come to me, she'd bring me something to wear. I hear say, sir, that I've died, and that this is heaven. I don't know why she hasn't come to me. Everybody else here seems to have somebody to meet him but me."

" 'This is not heaven," said the man.

A long silence followed. "It's not hell, is it?" said Sandy, at last.

The man apparently did not choose to answer the question. "Come," said he, "you waste time in talk. Get up. Wrap the sheet around you, and come with me."

"Where are you going to take me?" said Sandy.

"No matter," said the other. "Do as I tell you." His voice was calm, dispassionate; there was nothing of anger in it, but there was that which said he must be obeyed.

Sandy drew the sheet upon which he lay about him, and then shuddering, half with nervous dread and half with cold, arose from the warm bed in which he lay.

The other turned, and without saying a word led the way down the length of the room, Sandy following close behind. The noise of talking ceased as they passed by the various beds, and all turned

and looked after the two, some smiling,
some laughing outright. Sandy, as he
marched down the length of the room,
heard the rustling laugh and felt an echo
of the same dull humiliation he had felt
when he had marched with the other
guests of the East Haven Refuge to their
daily task of paving Main Street. There
as now the people laughed, and there in
the same manner as they did now; and
as he had there slouched in the body, so
now he slouched heavily in the spirit
after his conductor.

Opposite the end of the room where
was the door through which the friends
and visitors came and went was another
door, low and narrow. Sandy's guide led
the way directly to it, lifted the latch,
and opened it. It led to a long entry beyond, gloomy and dark. This passageway was dully lighted by a small square
window, glazed with clouded glass, at the
further end of the narrow hall, upon
which fronted a row of closed doors. The
place was very damp and chill; a cold
draught of air blew through the length
of it, and Sandy, as the other closed the
door through which they had just entered, and so shut out the noise beyond,
heard distinctly the sound of running
water. Without turning to the left or

to the right, Sandy's guide led the way down the hall, stopping at last when he had reached a door near the further end. He drew a bunch of keys from his pocket, chose one from among them, fitted it into the lock, and turned it.

"Go in there," said he, "and wash yourself clean, and then you shall have clothes to wear."

Sandy entered, and the door was closed behind him. The place in which he found himself was very cold, and the floor beneath his feet was wet and slimy. His teeth chattered and his limbs shuddered as he stood looking around him. The noise of flowing water sounded loud and clear through the silence; it was running from a leaden pipe into a wooden tank, mildewed and green with mould, that stood in the middle of the room. The stone - walls around, once painted white, were now also stained and splotched with great blotches of green and russet dampness. The only light that lit the place came in through a small, narrow, slatted window close to the ceiling, and opposite the doorway which he had entered. It was all gloomy, ugly, repellent.

There were some letters painted in red at the head of the wooden tank. He came

forward and read them, not without some
difficulty, for they were nearly erased.

This is the water of death!

Sandy started back so suddenly that
he nearly fell upon the slippery floor. A
keen pang of sudden terror shot through
him; then a thought that some grotesque
mockery was being played upon him. A
second thought blew the first away like a
breath of smoke, for it told him that
there could be no mockery in the place
to which he had come. His waking and
all that had happened to him had much
of nightmare grotesquery about it, but
there was no grotesquery or no appearance of jesting about that man who had
guided him to the place in which he now
found himself. There was a calm, impassive, unemotional sternness about all
that he said and did—official, automa-
tonlike—that precluded the possibility of
any jest or meaningless form. This must
indeed be the *water of death,* and his
soul told him that it was meant for
him.

He turned dully, and walked with
stumbling steps to the door. He felt
blindly for a moment for the latch, then
his hand touched it, and he raised it with
a click. The sharp sound jarred through
the silence, and Sandy did not open the

door. He stood for a little while staring
stupidly down upon the floor with his
palm still upon the latch. Was the man
who had brought him there waiting outside? Behind him lay the *water of death,*
but he dared not open the door and
chance the facing of that man. The sheet
had fallen away from him, and now he
stood entirely naked. He let the latch
fall back to its place—carefully, lest it
should again make a noise, and that man
should hear it. Then he gathered the
now damp and dirty sheet about him,
and crouched down upon the cold floor
close to the crack of the door.

There he sat for a while, every now
and then shuddering convulsively with
cold and terror, then by-and-by he began
to cry.

There is something abjectly, almost
brutally, pathetic in the ugly squalor of
a man's tears. Sandy Graff crying, and
now and then wiping his eyes with the
damp and dirty street, was almost a
more ugly sight than he had been in the
maudlin bathos of his former drunken-
ness.

So he sat for a long time, until finally
his crying ended, only for a sudden sob
now and then, and he only crouched,
wondering dully. At last he slowly arose,

gathering the sheet still closer around
him, and creeping step by step to the
tank, looked down into its depth. The
water was as clear as crystal; he dipped
his hand into it—it was as cold as ice.
Then he dropped aside the sheet, and
stood as naked as the day he was born.
He stepped into the water.

A deathly faintness fell upon him, and
he clutched at the edge of the tank; but
even as he clutched his sight failed, and
he felt himself sinking down into the
depths.

"Help!" he cried, hoarsely; and then
the water closed blackly over his head.

He felt himself suddenly snatched
out from the tank, warm towels were
wrapped about him, his limbs were
rubbed with soft linen, and at last he
opened his eyes. He still heard the
sound of running water, but now the
place in which he was was no longer
dark and gloomy. Some one had flung
open the slatted window, and a great
beam of warm, serene sunlight streamed
in, and lay in a dazzling white square
upon the wet floor. Two men were busied
about him. They had wrapped his body

in a soft warm blanket, and were wiping
dry his damp, chilled, benumbed hands
and feet.

"What does this mean?" said Sandy,
faintly. "Was I not then to die, after all? Was not that the *water of
death?*"

"*The water of death?*" said they.
"You did not read the words aright;
that was *the water of life.*" They helped
him dress himself in his clothes—clothes
not unlike those which the East Haven
Refuge had given its outgoing guests,
only, somehow, these did not make him
feel humiliated and abased as those had
made him feel. Then they led him out
of that place. They traversed the same
long passageway through which he had
come before, and so came to the bedroom
which he had left. The tenants were all
gone now, and the attendants were busied
spreading the various beds with clean
linen sheets and coverlets, as though for
fresh arrivals.

No one seemed to pay any attention
to him. His conductors led the way to
the anteroom which Sandy had seen beyond.

A woman was sitting patiently looking
out of the window. She turned her head
as they entered, and Sandy, when he saw

her face, stood suddenly still, as though turned to stone. *It was his wife!*

VI

With Colonel Singelsby was no such nightmare awakening as with Sandy Graff; with him were no such ugly visions and experiences; with him was no squalor and discomfort. Yet he also opened his eyes upon a room so like that upon which they had closed that at first he thought that he was still in the world. There was the same soft bed, the same warmth of ease and comfort, the same style of old-fashioned furniture. There were the curtained windows, the pictures upon the wall, the bright warm fire burning in the grate.

At first he saw all these things drowsily, as one does upon newly awakening. With him, as with Sandy, it was only when his conscious life had opened wide and clear enough to observe and to recognize who they were that were gathered around him that with a keen, almost agonizing thrill he realized where he was and what had befallen him. Upon one side of his bed stood his son Hubert; upon the other side stood his brother

James. The one had died ten, the other
nineteen years before. Of all those who
had gone from the world which he himself had just left, these stood the nearest
to him, and now, in his resurrection, his
opening eyes first saw these two. They
and other relatives and friends helped
him to arise and dress, as Sandy had seen
the poor wretches in the place in which
he had awakened raised from their beds
and dressed by their friends.

All Colonel Singelsby's teachings had
told him that this was not so different
from the world he had left behind. Nevertheless, although he was prepared
somewhat for it, it was wonderful to
him how alike the one was to the other.
The city, the streets, the people coming
and going, the stores, the parks, the great
houses—all were just as they were in the
world of men. He had no difficulty in
finding his way about the streets. There,
in comfortable houses of a better class,
were many of his friends; others were
not to be found; some, he was told, had
ascended higher; others, he was also told,
had descended lower.

Among other places, Colonel Singelsby found himself during the afternoon
in the house of one with whom he had

been upon friendly, almost intimate
terms in times past in the world. Colonel
Singelsby remembered hearing that the
good man had died a few months before
he himself had left the world. He wondered what had become of him, and then
in a little while he found himself in his
old friend's house. It had been many
years since he had seen him. He remembered him as a benign, venerable old
gentleman, and he had been somewhat
surprised to find that he was still living
in the town, instead of having ascended
to a higher state.

The old gentleman still looked outwardly venerable, still outwardly benign,
but now there was under his outer seeming a somewhat of restless querulous-
ness, a something of uneasy discontent,
that Colonel Singelsby did not remember
to have seen there before. They talked
together about many things, chiefly of
those in the present state of existence in
which they found themselves. It was all
very new and vivid upon Colonel Singelsby's mind, but the reverend gentleman seemed constantly to forget that he
was in another world than that which
he had left behind. It seemed to be always with an effort that he brought himself to talk of the world in which he lived

as the world of spirits. The visit was
somehow unpleasant to Colonel Singelsby. He was impressed with a certain air
of intolerance exhibited by the other.
His mind seemed to dwell more upon the
falsity of the old things than upon the
truth of the new, and he seemed to take
a certain delight in showing how and in
what everybody but those of his own
creed erred and fell short of the Di-
vine intent, and not the least disagreeable part of the talk to Colonel Singelsby was that the other's words seemed to find a sort of echo in his own
mind.

At last he proposed a walk, and the
other, taking his hat and stick, accompanied him for a little distance upon the
way. The talk still clung much to the
same stem to which it had adhered all
along.

"It is a very strange thing," said the
reverend gentleman, "but a great many
people who have come to this town since
I came hither have left it again to
ascend, as I have been told, to a higher
state. I think there must have been
some mistake, for I cannot see how it is
possible—and in fact our teachings distinctly tell us that it is impossible—for
one to ascend to a higher state without

having accepted the new truths of the
new order of things."

Colonel Singelsby did not make answer. He was not only growing tired of
the subject itself, but of his old friend
as well.

They were at that moment crossing an
angle of a small park shaded by thin,
spindly trees. As the Colonel looked up
he saw three men and a woman approaching along the same path and under the flickering shadows. Two of the
men walked a little in advance, the other
walked with the woman. There was
something familiar about two of the
group, and Colonel Singelsby pointed at
them with his finger.

"Who are they?" said he. "I am sure
there is somebody I know."

The other adjusted his glasses and
looked. "I do not know," said he, "except that one of the men is a new-comer.
We somehow grow to know who are new-
comers by the time we have lived here a
little while."

"Dear me!" cried Colonel Singelsby,
stopping abruptly, "I know that man. I
did not know that he had come here too.
I wonder where they are going?"

"I think," said the reverend gentleman, dryly—"I think that this is one

of those cases of which I just spoke to
you. I judge from the general appearance of the party that they are about to
ascend, as they call it here, to a higher
state."

"That is impossible!" said Colonel
Singelsby. "That man is a poor wretched creature whom I have helped with
charity again and again, it cannot be
that he is to go to a higher state, for he
is not fit for it. If he is to be taken
anywhere, it must be to punishment."

The other shrugged his shoulders and
said nothing, he had seen such cases too
often during his sojourn to be deceived.

The little party had now come close to
the two, and Colonel Singelsby stepped
forward with all his old-time frank kind-
ness of manner. "Why, Sandy," said he,
"I did not know that you also had come
here."

"Yes, sir," said Sandy; "I died the
same night you did."

"Dear me!" said the Colonel, "that is
very singular, very singular indeed!
Where are you going now, Sandy?"

"I don't know," said Sandy; "these
gentlemen here are taking me somewhere,
I don't know where. This is my wife,"
said he. "Don't you remember her,
sir?"

"Oh yes," said the Colonel, with his most pleasant air, "I remember her very well, but of course I am not so much surprised to see her here as I am to see you. But have you no idea where you are going?" he continued.

"No," said Sandy; "but perhaps these gentlemen can tell you." And he looked inquiringly at his escort, who stood calmly listening to what was said.

So far, the Parable, as I had read it, progressed onward with some coherence and concatenation, a coherence and concatenation growing perhaps more disjointed as it advanced. Now it began to be broken with interjectory sentences, and just here was one, the tenor of which I could not altogether understand, but have since comprehended more or less clearly. I cannot give its exact words, but only its general form.

"O wretched man," it said, "how pitiful are thy vain efforts and strivings to keep back by thine own strength that fiery flood of hell which grows and increases to overwhelm thy soul! If the inflowing of good which Jehovah vouchsafes is infinite, only less infinite is the outflowing of that which thou callest evil and wickedness. How, then, canst thou

*hope to stand against it and to conquer?
How canst thou hope to keep back that
raging torrent of fire and of flame with
the crumbling unbaked bricks of thine
own soul's making? Poor fool! Thou
mayst endeavor, thou mayst strive, thou
mayst build thy wall of defence higher
and higher, fearing God, and living a life
of virtue, but by-and-by thou wilt reach
the end, and then wilt find thou canst
build no higher! Then how vain shall
have been thy life of resistance! First
that flood shall trickle over the edge of
thy defence; then it shall run a stream
the breadth of a man's hand; then it
shall gush forth a torrent; then, bursting
over and through and around, it shall
sweep away all that thou hast so laboriously built up, and shall rush, howling,
roaring, raging, and burning through thy
soul with ten thousand times the fury
and violence that it would have done if
thou hadst not striven to keep it back,
if thou hadst not resisted and fought
against it. For bear this in mind: Christ
said he came not to call the good to re-
pentence, but the evil, and if thou art
full of thine own, how then canst thou
hope to receive of a God that asketh not
for sacrifice, but for love?"*

Hence again the story resumed.

Colonel Singelsby had not before noticed the two men who were with Sandy, now he observed them more closely. They were tall, middle-aged men, with serious, placid, unemotional faces. Each carried a long white staff, the end of which rested upon the ground. There was about them something somehow different from anything Coloned Singelsby had ever seen before. They were most quiet, courteous men, but there was that in their personal appearance that was singularly unpleasant to Colonel Singelsby. Why, he could not tell, for they were evidently gentlemen, and, from their bearing, men of influence. He turned to Sandy again.

"How has it been with you since you have been here?" said he.

"It has been very hard with me," said Sandy, patiently; "very hard indeed; but I hope and believe now that the worst is over, and that by-and-by I shall be happy, and not have any more trouble."

"I trust so, indeed," said the Colonel; "but do not hope for too much, Sandy. Even the best men coming to this world are not likely to be rid of their troubles at once, and it is not to be hoped for that you, after your ill-spent life, should find your lot easier than theirs."

"I know, sir," said Sandy, "and I am very sorry."

There was a meek acceptance of the Colonel's dictum that grated somehow unpleasantly upon the Colonel's ears. He would rather that Sandy had made some protest against that dictum. He approached half a step and looked more keenly at the other, and then for the first time he saw that some great, some radical, some tremendous change had happened. The man before him was no doubt Sandy Graff, but all that was low-browed, evil, foul, was gone, as though it had been washed away, and in its place was a translucent, patient meekness, almost like— There was something so terribly vital in that change that Colonel Singelsby shuddered before it. He looked and looked, and then he passed the back of his hand across his eyes. "All this is very unreal," said he, turning to his friend the minister. "It is like a dream. I begin to feel as though nothing was real. Surely it is not possible that magic changes can go on, and yet I cannot understand all these things in the least."

For answer, the reverend gentleman shrugged his shoulders almost sourly.

"Gentlemen," said Colonel Singelsby,

turning abruptly upon Sandy's escort, "let me ask you is this a certain man whom I used to know as Sandy Graff?"

One of the men nodded his head.

"And will you tell me," said he, "another thing? Will you kindly tell me where you are taking him?"

"We are about to take him," said the man, looking steadily at the Colonel as he answered—"we are about to take him to the outskirts of the First Kingdom."

At the answer Colonel Singelsby actually fell back a pace in his amazement. It was almost as though a blow had fallen upon him. "The outskirts of the First Kingdom?" said he. "Did I understand you? The outskirts of the First Kingdom? Surely there is some mistake here! It is not possible that this man, who died only yesterday, filthy and polluted with iniquity, stinking in the nostrils of God with ten thousand indulged and gratified lusts—it is not possible that you intend taking him to that land, passing by me, who all my life have lived to my best endeavors in love to God and my neighbor?"

It was the voice of his minister that broke the answer. "Yes, they do," said he, sharply; "that is just what they do mean. They do mean to take him, and they do mean to leave us, for such is the law in this dreadful place. We, the children of light, are nothing, and they, the fuel of hell, are everything. Have I not been telling you so?"

Colonel Singelsby had almost forgotten the presence of his acquaintance. He felt very angry at his interference, and somehow he could no longer govern his anger as he used to do. He turned upon him and fixed him with a frown, and then he observed for the first time that a little crowd had begun gathering, and now stood looking on, some curious and unsmiling, some grinning. The Colonel drew himself to his height, and looked haughtily about him. They who grinned began laughing. And now, at last, it was come Colonel Singelsby's turn to feel as Sandy Graff had felt—as though all that was happening to him was happening in some hideous nightmare dream. As in a dream, the balancing weights of reasoning and morality began to melt before the heat of that which burned within; as in a dream, the uncurbed inner motives began to strive furiously. Then a sudden fierce anger, quite like the savage irrational anger of an ugly dream, flamed up quickly and fiercely. He opened his lips as though to vent his rage, but for an instant his tottering reason regained a momentary poise. Checking himself with an effort ten thousand times greater than that he would have used in his former state and in the world, he bowed his head upon his breast and stood for a little while with fingers interlocked, clinching his trembling hands together. So he stood for a while, brooding, until at last Sandy and his escort made a motion as if to pass by. Then he spoke again.

"Stop a bit!" said he, looking up— "stop a bit!" His voice was hoarse and constrained, and he looked neither to the right nor to the left, but straight at that one of the men to whom he had spoken before. "Sir," said he, and then clearing his husky voice—"sir," again, "I have learned a lesson—the greatest lesson of my life! I have looked into my heart, and I have seen—I have seen myself— God help me, gentlemen!—I—maybe I am no better than this man."

The crowd, which had been increasing, as crowds do, began to jeer at the words, for, like most crowds, it was of a nether sort, and enjoyed the unusual sight of the gentleman and the aristocrat abasing and humiliating himself before the reformed drunkard.

At the sound of that ugly jeering

laugh Colonel Singelsby quivered as
though under the cut of a lancet, but he
never removed his eyes from the man to
whom he spoke. For a moment or two
he bit his nether lip in his effort for
self-control, and then repeated, in a
louder and perhaps harsher voice, "I am
no better than this man!" He paused
for a moment, and the crowd ceased its
jeering to hear what he had to say. "I
ask only this," he said, "that you will
take me where you are taking him, and
that I may enjoy such happiness as he
is about to enjoy."

Instantly a great roar of laughter went
up from the crowd, which had now gathered to some twenty or thirty souls. The
man to whom Colonel Singelsby had
spoken shook his head calmly and im-
passively.

"It cannot be," said he.

Colonel Singelsby turned white to the
very lips, his eyes blazed, and his breath
came thick and heavily. His nostrils
twitched spasmodically, but still, with a
supreme effort — a struggle so terrible
that few men happily may ever know it
or experience it—he once more controlled
the words that sprang to his lips and
struggled for utterance. He swallowed
and swallowed convulsively. "Sir," said

he at last, in a voice so hoarse, so horribly constrained, that it seemed almost to rend him as it forced utterance—"sir, surely I am mistaken in what I understand; it is little I ask you, and surely not unjust. Yesterday this man was a vile, debauched drunkard; surely that does not make him fitter for heaven! Yesterday I was a God-fearing, law-abiding man, surely that does not make me unfit! I am not unfit, am I?"

"You are not yet fit for heaven," answered the man, with impassive calmness. And again, for the third time, the crowd roared with evil laughter.

Within Colonel Singelsby's soul that fiery flood was now lashing dreadfully close to the summit of its barriers. His face was as livid as death, and his hands were clinched till the nails cut into his palm. "Let me understand for once and for all, for I confess I cannot understand all this. You say he is to go, and that I am not to go! Is it, then, God's will and God's justice that because this man for twenty years has led a life of besotted sin and indulgence, and because I for sixty years have feared God and loved my neighbor, that he is to be chosen and I am to be left?"

The man did not reply in words, but

in the steady look of his unwinking eyes
the other read his answer.

"Then," gasped Colonel Singelsby, and
as he spoke he shook his clinched and
trembling fist against the still, blue sky
overhead—"then, if that be God's justice, may it be damned, for I want none
of it."

Then came the end, swiftly, completely. For the fourth time the crowd
laughed, and at the sound those flood-
gates so laboriously built up during a
lifetime of abstinence were suddenly
burst asunder and fell crashing, and a
burning flood of hell's own rage and
madness rushed roaring and thundering
into his depleted, empty soul, flaming,
blazing, consuming like straws every pre-
cept of righteousness, every fear of God,
and Colonel Edward Singelsby, the one-
time Christian gentleman, the one-time
upright son of grace, the one-time man
of law and God, was transformed instantly and terribly into—what? Was it
a livid devil from hell? He cursed the
jeering crowd, and at the sound of his
own curses a blindness fell upon him,
and he neither knew what he said nor
what he did. His good old friend, who
had accompanied him so far and until
now had stood by him, suddenly turned,

and maybe fearing lest some thunder-
bolt of vengeance should fall upon them
from heaven and consume them all, he
elbowed himself out of the crowd and
hurried away. As for the wretched mad-
man, in his raging fury, it was not the
men who had forbidden him heaven
whom he strove to rend and tear limb
from limb, but poor, innocent, harmless
Sandy Graff. The crowd swayed and
jostled this way and that, and as madness begets madness, the curses that fell
from one pair of lips found an echo in
curses that leaped from others. Sandy
shrunk back appalled before the hell-
blast that breathed upon him, and he
felt his wife clutch him closer. Only two
of those that were there stood unmoved;
they were the two men who acted as
Sandy's escort. As the tide of madness
seemed to swell higher, they calmly
stepped forward and, crossed their staves
before their charge. There was something in their action full of significance
for those who knew. Instantly the crowd
melted away like snow under a blast of
fire. Had there not been two men present
more merciful than the rest, it is hard
to say what terrible thing might not
have happened to Colonel Edward Singelsby — deaf and dumb and blind to

everything but his own rage. These two clutched him by the arms and dragged him back.

"God, man!" they cried, "what are you doing? Do you not see they are angels?"

They dragged him back to a bench that stood near, and there held him, whilst he still beat the air with his fist and cried out hoarse curses, and even as they so held him, two other men came—two men dark, silent, sinister—and led him away.

Then the other and his wife and his two escorts passed by and out of the gate of the town, and away towards the mountain that stood still and blue in the distance.

So far I read, and then I could bear to read no more, but placed my hand upon the open page of the book. "What is this dreadful thing?" I cried. "Is, then, a man punished for truth and justice and virtue and righteousness? Is it, then, true that the evil are rewarded, and that the good are punished so dreadfully?"

Then the man who held the book spoke again. "Take away thy hand and read," said he.

Then I took away my hand, and read as he bade me, and found these words:

"*How can God fill with His own that which is already filled by man? First it must be emptied before it may be filled with the true good of righteousness and truth, of humility and love, of peace and joy. O thou foolish one who judgest but from the appearance of things, how long will it be before thou canst understand that while some may be baptized with water to cleanliness and repentance, others are baptized with living fire to everlasting life, and that they alone are the children of God?*"

Then again I read these words:

"*Woe to thee, thou who deniest the laws of God and man! Woe to thee, thou who walkest in the darkness of the shadow of sin and evil! But ten thousand times woe to thee, thou who pilest Pelion of self-good upon Ossa of self-truth, not that thou mayst scale therefrom the gate of Heaven, but that thou mayst hide thyself beneath from the eye of the Living God! By-and-by His Day shall come! His Terrible Lightning shall flash from the East to the West! His Dreadful Flaming Thunder-bolt shall fall, riving thy secret fastnesses to atoms, and leaving thee, poor worm,*

*writhing in the dazzling effulgence of
His Light, and shrivelling beneath the
consuming flame of His Loving-kind-
ness!"*

*Then the leaf was turned, and there
before me lay the answer to that first
question, "What shall a man do that
he may gain the kingdom of Heaven?"
There stood the words, plain and clear.
But I did not dare to read them, but
turning, left that place, shutting the door
to behind me.*

*Never have I found that door or en-
tered that room again, but by-and-by I
know that I shall find them both once
more, and shall then and there read the
answer that forever stands written in
that book, for it still lies open at the
very page, and he upon whose knees it
rests is Israfeel, the Angel of Death.*

But what of the sequel? Is there a
sequel? Are we, then, to suffer ourselves
to do evil for the sake of shunning pain
in the other world? I trow not! He
who sets his foot to climb must never
look backward and downward. He who
suffers most must reach the highest.
There must be another part of the story
which lies darkly and dimly behind the
letter. One can see, faintly and dimly

but nevertheless clearly, what the poor
man was to enjoy—the poor man who
from without appeared to be so evil, and
yet within was not really evil. One can
see a vision faint and dim of a simple
little house cooled by the dewy shade of
green trees forever in foliage; one can
see pleasant meadows and gardens forever green, stretching away to the banks
of a smooth-flowing river in whose level
bosom rests a mirrored image of that
which lies beyond its farther bank—a
great town with glistering walls and
gleaming spires reaching tower above
tower and height above height into the
blazing blue, the awful serenity of a
heavenly sky. One can know that toward that town the poor man who had
sinned and repented would in the evenings gaze and wonder until his soul, now
ploughed clean for new seed, might learn
the laws that would make it indeed an
inhabitant of that place. It is a serene
and beautiful vision, but not different
from that which all may see, and enjoy
even, in part, in this world.

But how was it with that other man
—with that good man who had never
sinned until his earthly body was
stripped away that he might sin and fall
in the spirit—sin and fall to a depth so

profound that even one furtive look into
that awful abysm makes the minds of
common men to reel and stagger? When
that God-sent blast of fire should have
burned out the selfhood that clung to
the very vitals of his soul, what then?
Who is there that with unwinking eyes
may gaze into the effulgent brilliancy of
the perfect angelhood? He who sweats
drops of salt in his life's inner struggles
shall, maybe, eat good bread in the dew
of it, but he who sweats drops of blood
in agony shall, when his labor is done,
sit him, maybe, at the King's table, and
feast upon the Flesh of Life and the very
Wine of Truth.

Was it so with that man who never
sinned until all his hell was let loose at
once upon him?

The Little Room

BY MADELENE YALE WYNNE

"HOW would it do for a smoking-room?"

"Just the very place; only, you know, Roger, you must not think of smoking in the house. I am almost afraid having just a plain common man around, let alone a smoking-man, will upset Aunt Hannah. She is New England — Vermont New England boiled down."

"You leave Aunt Hannah to me; I shall find her tender side. I am going to ask her about the old sea-captain and the yellow calico."

"Not yellow calico—blue chintz."

"Well, yellow *shell,* then."

"No, no! don't mix it up so; you won't know yourself what to expect, and that's half the fun."

"Now you tell me again exactly what to expect; to tell the truth, I didn't half hear about it the other day; I was wool-

gathering. It was something queer that
happened when you were a child, wasn't
it ?"

" Something that began to happen long
before that, and kept happening, and may
happen again; but I hope not."

" What was it ?"

" I wonder if the other people in the
car can hear us ?"

" I fancy not; we don't hear them—not
consecutively, at least."

" Well, mother was born in Vermont,
you know; she was the only child by a
second marriage. Aunt Hannah and
Aunt Maria are only half-aunts to me,
you know."

" I hope they are half as nice as you
are."

" Roger, be still; they certainly will
hear us."

" Well, don't you want them to know
we are married ?"

" Yes, but not just married. There's
all the difference in the world."

" You are afraid we look too happy !"

" No; only I want my happiness all to
myself."

" Well, the little room ?"

" My aunts brought mother up; they
were nearly twenty years older than she.
I might say Hiram and they brought her

up. You see, Hiram was bound out to
my grandfather when he was a boy, and
when grandfather died Hiram said he
' s'posed he went with the farm, 'long o'
the critters,' and he has been there ever
since. He was my mother's only refuge
from the decorum of my aunts. They
are simply workers. They make me think
of the Maine woman who wanted her epi-
taph to be, 'She was a *hard* working
woman.' "

" They must be almost beyond their
working-days. How old are they ?"

" Seventy, or thereabouts; but they
will die standing; or, at least, on a Saturday night, after all the house-work is
done up. They were rather strict with
mother, and I think she had a lonely
childhood. The house is almost a mile
away from any neighbors, and off on top
of what they call Stony Hill. It is bleak
enough up there even in summer.

" When mamma was about ten years
old they sent her to cousins in Brooklyn,
who had children of their own, and knew
more about bringing them up. She stayed
there till she was married; she didn't go
to Vermont in all that time, and of
course hadn't seen her sisters, for they
never would leave home for a day. They
couldn't even be induced to go to Brook-

lyn to her wedding, so she and father took their wedding-trip up there."

"And that's why we are going up there on our own?"

"Don't, Roger; you have no idea how loud you speak."

"You never say so except when I am going to say that one little word."

"Well, don't say it, then, or say it very, very quietly."

"Well, what was the queer thing?"

"When they got to the house, mother wanted to take father right off into the little room; she had been telling him about it, just as I am going to tell you, and she had said that of all the rooms, that one was the only one that seemed pleasant to her. She described the furniture and the books and paper and everything, and said it was on the north side, between the front and back room. Well, when they went to look for it, there was no little room there; there was only a shallow china-closet. She asked her sisters when the house had been altered and a closet made of the room that used to be there. They both said the house was exactly as it had been built—that they had never made any changes, except to tear down the old wood - shed and build a smaller one.

9   S. H. D.

"Father and mother laughed a good deal over it, and when anything was lost they would always say it must be in the little room, and any exaggerated statement was called 'little-roomy.' When I was a child I thought that was a regular English phrase, I heard it so often.

"Well, they talked it over, and finally they concluded that my mother had been a very imaginative sort of a child, and had read in some book about such a little room, or perhaps even dreamed it, and then had 'made believe,' as children do, till she herself had really thought the room was there."

"Why, of course, that might easily happen."

"Yes, but you haven't heard the queer part yet; you wait and see if you can explain the rest as easily.

"They stayed at the farm two weeks, and then went to New York to live. When I was eight years old my father was killed in the war, and mother was broken-hearted. She never was quite strong afterwards, and that summer we decided to go up to the farm for three months.

"I was a restless sort of a child, and the journey seemed very long to me; and

finally, to pass the time, mamma told me
the story of the little room, and how it
was all in her own imagination, and how
there really was only a china-closet there.

"She told it with all the particulars;
and even to me, who knew beforehand
that the room wasn't there, it seemed just
as real as could be. She said it was on
the north side, between the front and back
rooms; that it was very small, and they
sometimes called it an entry. There was
a door also that opened out-of-doors, and
that one was painted green, and was cut
in the middle like the old Dutch doors,
so that it could be used for a window by
opening the top part only. Directly opposite the door was a lounge or couch;
it was covered with blue chintz—India
chintz—some that had been brought over
by an old Salem sea-captain as a 'vent-
ure.' He had given it to Maria when she
was a young girl. She was sent to Salem
for two years to school. Grandfather
originally came from Salem."

"I thought there wasn't any room or
chintz."

"*That is just it.* They had decided
that mother had imagined it all, and yet
you see how exactly everything was painted in her mind, for she had even remembered that Hiram had told her that Maria

could have married the sea-captain if
she had wanted to!

"The India cotton was the regular
blue-stamped chintz, with the peacock figure on it. The head and body of the bird
were in profile, while the tail was full
front view behind it. It had seemed to
take mamma's fancy, and she drew it for
me on a piece of paper as she talked.
Doesn't it seem strange to you that she
could have made all that up, or even
dreamed it?

"At the foot of the lounge were some
hanging-shelves with some old books on
them. All the books were leather-colored
except one; that was bright red, and was
called the *Ladies' Album*. It made a
bright break between the other thicker
books.

"On the lower shelf was a beautiful
pink sea-shell, lying on a mat made of
balls of red-shaded worsted. This shell
was greatly coveted by mother, but she
was only allowed to play with it when
she had been particularly good. Hiram
had showed her how to hold it close to
her ear and hear the roar of the sea in it.

"I know you will like Hiram, Roger,
he is quite a character in his way.

"Mamma said she remembered, or
thought she remembered, having been

sick once, and she had to lie quietly for
some days on the lounge; then was the
time she had become so familiar with
everything in the room, and she had been
allowed to have the shell to play with all
the time. She had had her toast brought
to her in there, with make-believe tea. It
was one of her pleasant memories of her
childhood; it was the first time she had
been of any importance to anybody, even
herself.

" Right at the head of the lounge was
a light-stand, as they called it, and on it
was a very brightly polished brass candle-
stick and a brass tray, with snuffers.
That is all I remember of her describing,
except that there was a braided rag rug
on the floor, and on the wall was a beautiful flowered paper — roses and morning-
glories in a wreath on a light-blue ground.
The same paper was in the front room."

" And all this never existed except in
her imagination ?"

" She said that when she and father
went up there, there wasn't any little
room at all like it anywhere in the house;
there was a china-closet where she had
believed the room to be."

" And your aunts said there had never
been any such room ?"

" That is what they said."

"Wasn't there any blue chintz in the house with a peacock figure?"

"Not a scrap, and Aunt Hannah said there had never been any that she could remember; and Maria just echoed her— she always does that. You see, Aunt Hannah is an up-and-down New England woman. She looks just like herself; I mean, just like her character. Her joints move up and down or backward and forward in a plain square fashion. I don't believe she ever leaned on anything in her life, or sat in an easy-chair. But Maria is different; she is rounder and softer; she hasn't any ideas of her own; she never had any. I don't believe she would think it right or becoming to have one that differed from Aunt Hannah's, so what would be the use of having any? She is an echo, that's all.

"When mamma and I got there, of course I was all excitement to see the china-closet, and I had a sort of feeling that it would be the little room after all. So I ran ahead and threw open the door, crying, 'Come and see the little room.'

"And, Roger," said Mrs. Grant, laying her hand in his, "there really was a little room there, exactly as mother had remembered it. There was the lounge, the peacock chintz, the green door, the shell, the morning-glory and rose paper, *every-thing exactly as she had described it to me.*"

"What in the world did the sisters say about it?"

"Wait a minute and I will tell you. My mother was in the front hall still talking with Aunt Hannah. She didn't hear me at first, but I ran out there and dragged her through the front room, saying, 'The room *is* here—it is all right.'

"It seemed for a minute as if my mother would faint. She clung to me in terror. I can remember now how strained her eyes looked and how pale she was.

"I called out to Aunt Hannah and asked her when they had had the closet taken away and the little room built; for in my excitement I thought that that was what had been done.

"'That little room has always been there,' said Aunt Hannah, 'ever since the house was built.'

"'But mamma said there wasn't any little room here, only a china-closet, when she was here with papa,' said I.

"'No, there has never been any china-closet there; it has always been just as it is now,' said Aunt Hannah.

"Then mother spoke; her voice sounded weak and far off. She said, slowly, and with an effort, 'Maria, don't you remember that you told me that there had *never been any little room here?* and Hannah said so too, and then I said I must have dreamed it?'

" 'No, I don't remember anything of the kind,' said Maria, without the slightest emotion. 'I don't remember you ever said anything about any china-closet. The house has never been altered; you used to play in this room when you were a child, don't you remember?'

" 'I know it,' said mother, in that queer slow voice that made me feel frightened. 'Hannah, don't you remember my finding the china-closet here, with the gilt-edge china on the shelves, and then *you* said that the *china-closet* had always been here?'

" 'No,' said Hannah, pleasantly but unemotionally—'no, I don't think you ever asked me about any china-closet, and we haven't any gilt-edged china that I know of.'

" And that was the strangest thing about it. We never could make them remember that there had ever been any question about it. You would think they could remember how surprised mother had been before, unless she had imagined

the whole thing. Oh, it was so queer!
They were always pleasant about it, but
they didn't seem to feel any interest or
curiosity. It was always this answer:
'The house is just as it was built; there
have never been any changes, so far as
we know.'

"And my mother was in an agony of
perplexity. How cold their gray eyes
looked to me! There was no reading anything in them. It just seemed to break
my mother down, this queer thing. Many
times that summer, in the middle of the
night, I have seen her get up and take a
candle and creep softly down-stairs. I
could hear the steps creak under her
weight. Then she would go through the
front room and peer into the darkness,
holding her thin hand between the candle and her eyes. She seemed to think
the little room might vanish. Then she
would come back to bed and toss about
all night, or lie still and shiver; it used
to frighten me.

"She grew pale and thin, and she had
a little cough; then she did not like to be
left alone. Sometimes she would make
errands in order to send me to the little
room for something—a book, or her fan,
or her handkerchief; but she would never
sit there or let me stay in there long, and

sometimes she wouldn't let me go in
there for days together. Oh, it was pitiful!"

"Well, don't talk any more about it,
Margaret, if it makes you feel so," said
Mr. Grant.

"Oh yes, I want you to know all about
it, and there isn't much more—no more
about the room.

"Mother never got well, and she died
that autumn. She used often to sigh, and
say, with a wan little laugh, 'There is
one thing I am glad of, Margaret: your
father knows now all about the little
room.' I think she was afraid I dis-
trusted her. Of course, in a child's way,
I thought there was something queer
about it, but I did not brood over it. I
was too young then, and took it as a
part of her illness. But, Roger, do you
know, it really did affect me. I almost
hate to go there after talking about it; I
somehow feel as if it might, you know, be
a china-closet again."

"That's an absurd idea."

"I know it; of course it can't be. I
saw the room, and there isn't any china-
closet there, and no gilt-edged china in
the house, either."

And then she whispered, "But, Roger,
you may hold my hand as you do now,

if you will, when we go to look for the
little room."

" And you won't mind Aunt Hannah's
gray eyes ?"

" I won't mind *anything.*"

It was dusk when Mr. and Mrs. Grant
went into the gate under the two old
Lombardy poplars and walked up the narrow path to the door, where they were
met by the two aunts.

Hannah gave Mrs. Grant a frigid but
not unfriendly kiss; and Maria seemed
for a moment to tremble on the verge of
an emotion, but she glanced at Hannah,
and then gave her greeting in exactly
the same repressed and non-committal
way.

Supper was waiting for them. On the
table was the *gilt-edged china.* Mrs.
Grant didn't notice it immediately, till
she saw her husband smiling at her over
his teacup; then she felt fidgety, and
couldn't eat. She was nervous, and kept
wondering what was behind her, whether
it would be a little room or a closet.

After supper she offered to help about
the dishes, but, mercy! she might as well
have offered to help bring the seasons
round; Maria and Hannah couldn't be
helped.

So she and her husband went to find

the little room, or closet, or whatever was
to be there.

Aunt Maria followed them, carrying
the lamp, which she set down, and then
went back to the dish-washing.

Margaret looked at her husband. He
kissed her, for she seemed troubled; and
then, hand in hand, they opened the door.
It opened into a *china-closet*. The shelves
were neatly draped with scalloped paper;
on them was the gilt-edged china, with
the dishes missing that had been used at
the supper, and which at that moment
were being carefully washed and wiped
by the two aunts.

Margaret's husband dropped her hand
and looked at her. She was trembling a
little, and turned to him for help, for
some explanation, but in an instant she
knew that something was wrong. A
cloud had come between them; he was
hurt; he was antagonized.

He paused for an appreciable instant,
and then said, kindly enough, but in a
voice that cut her deeply:

" I am glad this ridiculous thing is
ended; don't let us speak of it again."

" Ended!" said she. " How ended?"
And somehow her voice sounded to her
as her mother's voice had when she stood
there and questioned her sisters about the

little room. She seemed to have to drag her words out. She spoke slowly: "It seems to me to have only just begun in my case! It was just so with mother when she—"

"I really wish, Margaret, you would let it drop. I don't like to hear you speak of your mother in connection with it. It—" He hesitated, for was not this their wedding - day? "It doesn't seem quite the thing, quite delicate, you know, to use her name in the matter."

She saw it all now: *he didn't believe her.* She felt a chill sense of withering under his glance.

"Come," he added, "let us go out, or into the dining-room, somewhere, anywhere, only drop this nonsense."

He went out; he did not take her hand now—he was vexed, baffled, hurt. Had he not given her his sympathy, his attention, his belief—and his hand?—and she was fooling him. What did it mean? —she so truthful, so free from morbidness—a thing he hated. He walked up and down under the poplars, trying to get into the mood to go and join her in the house.

Margaret heard him go out; then she turned and shook the shelves; she reached her hand behind them and tried to push the boards away; she ran out of the house on to the north side and tried to find in the darkness, with her hands, a door, or some steps leading to one. She tore her dress on the old rose-tree, she fell and rose and stumbled, then she sat down on the ground and tried to think. What could she think—was she dreaming?

She went into the house and out into the kitchen, and begged Aunt Maria to tell her about the little room—what had become of it, when had they built the closet, when had they bought the gilt-edged china?

They went on washing dishes and drying them on the spotless towels with methodical exactness; and as they worked they said that there had never been any little room, so far as they knew; the china-closet had always been there, and the gilt-edged china had belonged to their mother, it had always been in the house.

"No, I don't remember that your mother ever asked about any little room," said Hannah. "She didn't seem very well that summer, but she never asked about any changes in the house; there hadn't ever been any changes."

There it was again: not a sign of inter-

est, curiosity, or annoyance, not a spark
of memory.

She went out to Hiram. He was telling Mr. Grant about the farm. She had
meant to ask him about the room, but
her lips were sealed before her husband.

Months afterwards, when time had les-
sened the sharpness of their feelings, they
learned to speculate reasonably about the
phenomenon, which Mr. Grant had accepted as something not to be scoffed
away, not to be treated as a poor joke,
but to be put aside as something inexplicable on any ordinary theory.

Margaret alone in her heart knew that
her mother's words carried a deeper significance than she had dreamed of at the
time. " One thing I am glad of, your
father knows now," and she wondered if
Roger or she would ever know.

Five years later they were going to
Europe. The packing was done; the children were lying asleep, with their travelling things ready to be slipped on for an
early start.

Roger had a foreign appointment. They
were not to be back in America for some
years. She had meant to go up to say
good-by to her aunts; but a mother of
three children intends to do a great many
things that never get done. One thing

she had done that very day, and as she
paused for a moment between the writing of two notes that must be posted before she went to bed, she said:

"Roger, you remember Rita Lash?
Well, she and Cousin Nan go up to the
Adirondacks every autumn. They are
clever girls, and I have intrusted to them
something I want done very much."

"They are the girls to do it, then, every
inch of them."

"I know it, and they are going to."

"Well?"

"Why, you see, Roger, that little
room—"

"Oh—"

"Yes, I was a coward not to go myself, but I didn't find time, because I
hadn't the courage."

"Oh! *that* was it, was it?"

"Yes, just that. They are going, and
they will write us about it."

"Want to bet?"

"No; I only want to know."

Rita Lash and Cousin Nan planned to
go to Vermont on their way to the Adirondacks. They found they would have
three hours between trains, which would
give them time to drive up to the Keys
farm, and they could still get to the

camp that night. But, at the last minute, Rita was prevented from going. Nan had to go to meet the Adirondack party, and she promised to telegraph her when she arrived at the camp. Imagine Rita's amusement when she received this message: " Safely arrived; went to the Keys farm; it is a little room."

Rita was amused, because she did not in the least think Nan had been there. She thought it was a hoax; but it put it into her mind to carry the joke further by really stopping herself when she went up, as she meant to do the next week.

She did stop over. She introduced herself to the two maiden ladies, who seemed familiar, as they had been described by Mrs. Grant.

They were, if not cordial, at least not disconcerted at her visit, and willingly showed her over the house. As they did not speak of any other stranger's having been so see them lately, she became confirmed in her belief that Nan had not been there.

In the north room she saw the roses and morning-glory paper on the wall, and also the door that should open into —what?

She asked if she might open it.

"Certainly," said Hannah; and Maria echoed, "Certainly."

She opened it, and found the china-closet. She experienced a certain relief; she at least was not under any spell. Mrs. Grant left it a china-closet; she found it the same. Good.

But she tried to induce the old sisters to remember that there had at various times been certain questions relating to a confusion as to whether the closet had always been a closet. It was no use; their stony eyes gave no sign.

Then she thought of the story of the sea - captain, and said, "Miss Keys, did you ever have a lounge covered with India chintz, with a figure of a peacock on it, given to you in Salem by a sea-captain, who brought it from India?"

"I dun'no' as I ever did," said Hannah. That was all. She thought Maria's cheeks were a little flushed, but her eyes were like a stone-wall.

She went on that night to the Adirondacks. When Nan and she were alone in their room she said. "By-the-way, Nan, what did you see at the farm-house? and how did you like Maria and Hannah?"

Nan didn't mistrust that Rita had been there, and she began excitedly to tell her all about her visit. Rita could almost

have believed Nan had been there if she
hadn't known it was not so. She let her
go on for some time, enjoying her enthu-
siasm, and the impressive way in which
she described her opening the door and
finding the "little room." Then Rita
said: "Now, Nan, that is enough fibbing.
I went to the farm myself on my way up
yesterday, and there is *no* little room, and
there *never* has been any; it is a china-
closet, just as Mrs. Grant saw it last."

She was pretending to be busy unpacking her trunk, and did not look up for a
moment; but as Nan did not say anything, she glanced at her over her shoulder. Nan was actually pale, and it was
hard to say whether she was most angry
or frightened. There was something of
both in her look. And then Rita began
to explain how her telegram had put her
in the spirit of going up there alone. She
hadn't meant to cut Nan out. She only
thought— Then Nan broke in: "It isn't
that; I am sure you can't think it is that.
But I went myself, and you did not go;
you can't have been there, for *it is a little room.*"

Oh, what a night they had! They
couldn't sleep. They talked and argued,
and then kept still for a while, only to
break out again, it was so absurd. They

both maintained that they had been there, but both felt sure the other one was either crazy or obstinate beyond reason. They were wretched; it was perfectly ridiculous, two friends at odds over such a thing; but there it was — "little room," "china-closet," — "china-closet," "little room."

The next morning Nan was tacking up some tarlatan at a window to keep the midges out. Rita offered to help her, as she had done for the past ten years. Nan's "No, thanks," cut her to the heart.

"Nan," said she, "come right down from that stepladder and pack your satchel. The stage leaves in just twenty minutes. We can catch the afternoon express train, and we will go together to the farm. I am either going there or going home. You better go with me."

Nan didn't say a word. She gathered up the hammer and tacks, and was ready to start when the stage came round.

It meant for them thirty miles of staging and six hours of train, besides crossing the lake; but what of that, compared with having a lie lying round loose between them! Europe would have seemed easy to accomplish, if it would settle the question.

At the little junction in Vermont they

found a farmer with a wagon full of
meal-bags. They asked him if he could
not take them up to the old Keys farm
and bring them back in time for the return train, due in two hours.

They had planned to call it a sketching trip, so they said, "We have been
there before, we are artists, and we might
find some views worth taking, and we
want also to make a short call upon the
Misses Keys."

"Did ye calculate to paint the old
house in the picture?"

They said it was possible they might do
so. They wanted to see it, anyway.

"Waal, I guess you are too late. The
house burnt down last night, and everything in it."

The Bringing of the Rose

BY HARRIET LEWIS BRADLEY

FOR certain subjects one of the most valuable works of reference in all Berlin was Miss Olivia Valentine's "Adress - buch," the contents of which were self - collected, self - tested, and abounded in extensive information concerning hotels and pensions, apartments and restaurants, families offering German home life with the language, instructors, and courses of lectures, doctors, dentists, dressmakers, milliners, the most direct way to Mendelssohn's grave in the Alte Dreifaltigkeits - Kirchhof, how to find lodgings in Baireuth during the Wagner festival, where to stay in Oberammergau, if it happened to be the year of the Passion Play, and so on, indefinitely.

Miss Valentine herself was a kind-hearted, middle-aged woman, who, as the result of much sojourning in foreign lands, possessed an intelligent knowledge of subjects likely to be of use to other

sojourners, and who was cordially ready
to share the same, according to the needs
of the season. If it were November, people came asking in what manner they
could take most profitable advantage of
a Berlin winter; if it were approaching
spring, they wanted addresses for Paris
or Switzerland or Italy. It was March
now and Sunday afternoon. Mr. Morris
Davidson sat by Miss Valentine's table,
the famous "Adress-buch" in his hand.
"I suppose you don't undertake starting
parties for heaven?" he said, opening the
book. "Ah! here it is—'Himmel und
Hölle.' I might have known it, you are
so thorough."

"If you read a little further," remarked Miss Valentine, "you will see
that 'Himmel und Hölle' is a German
game."

"Oh yes, I remember now; we play it
at our pension. It's that game where you
say 'thou' to the you-people, and 'you'
to the thou-people, and are expected to
address strange ladies whom you are
meeting for the first time as Klara and
Charlotte and Wilhelmine, with most em-
barrassing familiarity, and it is very stupid if the game happens to send you to
heaven. I wonder if there really is such
a locality? I've been thinking lately I

should like to go there; things don't seem
to agree with me very well here. I've
closed my books, walked the Thiergarten
threadbare, sleep twelve hours out of
twenty-four, do everything I've been told
to do, with no result whatever except to
grow duller." The young man yawned
as he spoke. "Do excuse me; I've come
to such a pass that I'm not able to look
any one in the face without yawning.
All things considered, I am afraid I
shouldn't be any better off in heaven.
I'm afraid I couldn't stand the people,
there must be so many of them. I want
to get away from people."

"I know exactly where to send you,"
said Miss Valentine. "I was thinking
about it when you came in. It isn't heaven, but it is very near it, and it also begins with H; and you are sure to like it
—that is, unless you object to the ghost."

"Oh, not in the least; only is the rest
of it all right? Things are not, general-
ly; either the drainage is bad or there is
a haunted room, and every one who sleeps
in it dies, and of course one cannot help
sleeping in it, just to see how it is going
to work."

"Nothing of the kind," returned Miss
Valentine; "the drainage is excellent;
and as for the haunted room, I once

shared it half a summer with a niece and namesake of mine, and we were never troubled by any unusual occurrence, and we are both in excellent health and likely to remain so. The ghost is reported to have a Mona Lisa face, to be dressed in black, with something white and fluffy at the neck and sleeves, gold bracelets, a neckless and ring of black pearls, and she carries a rose. If her appearance means death or misfortune, the rose is white; if she is only straying about in a friendly way, the rose is red.

"The place is called the Halden—the Hill-side. I have taken the precaution to state vaguely that it is in the neighborhood of Zurich; I want to do all in my power to keep the spot unspoiled. There is so little left in Switzerland that is not tired of being looked at—the trees are tired, and the grass, and the waterfalls; but here is a sweet hidden-away nook, where everything is as fresh as before the days of foreign travel. I am going to provide you with the directions for finding it."

She sat down by the writing-desk, and presently gave a slip of paper to Morris Davidson, who put it carefully in his pocket-book.

"The castle of the Halden," Miss Val-

entine continued, "belonged to a certain
countess, by name Maria Regina. There
is a tradition that one night a mist coming down from the mountain concealed the castle from the village, and when
it lifted, behold! the countess and her entire household had vanished forever, and
not a word was ever heard from them
again. The ghost-lady is supposed to be
a sister of the Countess Maria Regina,
and in some way connected with the
death of a young Austrian officer who
figures as a lover in the story; just
whose lover no one seems to know, but
it is surmised of Maria Regina's daughter, said to be a very aristocratic and
haughty young person. The castle remained closed after this mysterious occurrence for about two hundred years,
and then an enterprising Swiss-German
had it put in order for a summer hotel.
What are you doing? I believe you are
making extracts from my 'Adress-buch.'
Now that is something I never allow. I
like to give out information discriminate-
ly, with personal explanations."

The young man showed what he had
written. "Just a hint or two for Italy,"
he said. "I may go down there next
week. If I do, I shall certainly turn
aside and tarry a little at your Halden.

I should like to try whether your ghost-lady would lead me into any adventure."

Miss Valentine did not see Morris Davidson again, but a few weeks later she received a letter bearing a Swiss postmark:

"DEAR MISS VALENTINE,—I am here, and in order to give complete proof of it I sacrifice my prejudice and write on ruled paper, with purple ink and an unpleasant pen, that it may be all of the Halden. The place is exactly what I wanted and needed. I am so delighted to have it to myself. I am the only guest in the castle, the only stranger in the town. I came to stay a day; I intend now to stay a week. Yesterday, my first whole day, was perfect. I went by train to Mühlehorn, and walked from there to Wallenstadt, came back for dinner, and in the afternoon climbed the hill to Amden, where I found a hepatica in bloom, and had a beautiful view of the sunset. This morning there is a mist on the mountains, which is slowly rising, so I am using the time for letter-writing. Mountain-climbing is not yet inviting, owing to the snow; but, on the whole, the season of the year is not at all unfavorable. The loneliness is what I like best.

The people do not interest me; I avoid
them, and must appear in their eyes even
more deluded than I am to come to this
secluded spot at this unseasonable moment and be satisfied with my own society—no, not my own society, but that
of these kind brotherly mountains. From
a prosaic pedant I can almost feel myself becoming an ecstatical hermit, and
my soul getting ready to

'smooth itself out a long cramped scroll,
Freshening and fluttering in the wind.'

What a solid satisfaction it is to have a
few days free from railroad travel! I
have made a roundabout journey, coming
here by way of Dresden, Leipsic, Cologne,
Bonn, Frankfort, Heidelberg, Strasburg,
Freiburg, Basel, and Zurich. It was all
pleasant, but I am glad it is over. Please
never advertise the Halden as a health-
resort; let it remain a complete secret between us two, so that when we wish to
leave everything and hermitize we may
have the opportunity. If it were not
for betraying this secret, I should like to
recommend the castle for its generosity.
At breakfast I have put beside my plate
a five-pound loaf of bread, one slice of
which is fifteen inches long by six wide,
and thick *ad libitum* dimensions, the del-

icacy of which even a Prussian soldier
would call into question.

"I haven't attempted to tell you what
I think of your Halden. It is impossible.
I simply give myself over to a few days
of happiness and rest; all too soon I shall
have to face the busy world again.

"Most gratefully yours,
"MORRIS DAVIDSON.

"P.S.—I have not yet seen the ghost-
lady. I thought I heard her footstep last
night in the hall and a rustling at my
door. I opened it, half expecting to find
a rose upon the threshold. I found nothing, saw nothing."

The letter was dated March 13th, and
contained a pressed hepatica. Some two
months later another letter came. It
said:

"I am still here. My Italian journey melted into a Swiss sojourn. If I
stay much longer I shall not dare to
go away, I feel so safe under the care
of these wonderful mountains. What
words has one to describe them, with their
fulness of content, of majesty and mystery? I go daily up the time-worn steps
behind the castle, throw myself on the
grass, count the poplar-trees rising from

the plain below, try to make out where
earth ends and heaven begins as the white
May clouds meet the snow-drifts on the
mountain - tops. I am working a little
again, but tramping a good deal more. I
have not been so happy since I was a
boy. In a certain sense I have died here,
unaided by the apparition with the rose,
unless, indeed, she has come in my sleep,
and that of course would not count. I
have died, because surely all that death
can ever mean is the putting away of
something no longer needed, and therefore we die daily—one day most of all.
But although I have never seen the ghost-
lady, I have every reason to have perfect
faith in her existence. I was talking
with our landlord's aged mother about
it to-day. She carefully closed the door
when the conversation turned in this direction, begging me never to mention the
subject before the servants, and then in
a half-whisper she gave me exactly the
same description that you did in Berlin."

Early in June a third letter came:

"Will you believe me when I say I
have not only seen *Her*, but *Them;* that
I have sat with Them, and talked with
Them—the lost ladies of the Hill-side—

with the Countess Maria Regina, the
proud daughter, the mysterious sister?
No, certainly you will not believe me.

"I write nothing here of the physical
results of my stay. Enough that I am
ready for work; that I love my fellow-
men; that I no longer dread to go to heaven for fear of their society; that I have
formed an intimate friendship with the
village weaver and priest and postmaster;
that when we part, as we shall to-morrow, it will be affectionately and regret-
fully.

"All this you know, or have guessed.
What I am about to tell, you do not
know, and can never guess.

"It had been raining for a week. You
remember what it is like here when it
rains — how damp, sticky, discouraging;
how cold the stone floor; how wet the
fountain splashes when one goes through
the court to dinner. I was driven to
taking walks in the hall outside my room
by way of exercise, and thus discovered
in a certain dark corner a low door to
which I eventually succeeded in finding
a key. This door led me into an unused tower dimly lighted, hung with cobwebs, and filled with old red velvet
furniture. I sat down on a sofa, and
before long became conscious that I was

being gazed upon by a haughty young
woman, with an aristocratic nose, large
dark eyes, hair caught back by tortoise-
shell combs under a peculiar head-dress,
having a gleam of gold directly on the
top. Her gown was of dark green, with
white puffs let into the sleeves below
the elbows; around her tapering waist
was a narrow belt of jewels; the front
of her corsage was also trimmed with
jewels. But the most distinctive feature
of her costume consisted in a floating
scarf of old - rose, worn like the frontis-
piece lady in some volume of ' Keepsake '
or ' Token.' Imagine meeting such a being as this unexpectedly in the long-
closed tower-room of a castle after a week
of Swiss rain! I forgot time, weather,
locality, individuality; I began to think,
in fact, that I myself might be the young
Austrian officer who was murdered.
Presently I noticed that my haughty
young woman had a chaperon—a lady
wearing a light green picturesquely
shaped hood; a kerchief of the same shade
bordered with golden tassels; a necklace
of dark beads, from which hung a crucifix. She was not pretty, but had very
plump red cheeks, and held a little dog.
I learned, on nearer acquaintance, that
this was the Countess Maria Regina, and

as she then appeared so she had looked in the year 1695.

"We sat for a while silently regarding each other, Maria Regina's cheek seeming all the time to grow deeper in color, the point in which the green hood terminated more and more distinct, the little dog making ready to bark, the daughter with the floating scarf prouder and prouder, and I, as the Austrian officer, hardly daring to move, lest the sister with the rose should join the group, and that perhaps be the end of me, when I had the happy thought of going in search of her, and thus breaking the spell, and preventing the mischief which might occur should she come uninvited. I left the sofa and peered about, and could scarcely believe my eyes as I came upon her standing by the tower window, pearls, black gown, lace frills, and rose in hand, all there, although very indistinct and shadowy, the Mona Lisa face looking discreetly towards the wall.

"Now, my dear Miss Valentine, having related this remarkable adventure, I am about to relate one even more remarkable. It occurred this very evening, between seven and eight o'clock. I had been off for the day with the village goat-boy and his flock—the dear creatures, who

have never had their bells removed to be
painted over with Swiss landscapes and
offered for sale as souvenir bric-à-brac.
I had patted the goats good-night and
good-by, and going up to my room, thrown
myself into a reclining-chair, deliciously
tired as one can only be after a long day
of Swiss mountain life. The door was
open, the room full of pleasant twilight,
the three ladies safe in their tower close
by. I was thinking and wondering about
them, when I heard a rustling at the opposite end of the room. Now, as you
know, the place being spacious as a ban-
queting-hall, objects at a distance, especially in the half-light, might easily de-
ceive one. This was what I thought as I
saw by the window a girlish form in
black, with something white at the neck
and sleeves. I rubbed my hands across
my eyes, looked again, and, lo! my vision
had vanished completely, noiselessly, without moving from the spot; for there had
not been time to move. I sprang up
and crossed the room. On the window-
ledge was a rose, and the rose was red.

"Another curious thing — the ghost-
lady of the tower, according to her own
authority, was forty-nine in the year
1698. I don't know how ghosts manage
about their age, but my ghost of this

evening couldn't have been over nine-teen.

"Well, I have told my story. I wait for you to suggest the explanation of the second part; the first will explain itself when I bring to you, in a few days at most, and with the hearty consent and approval of the castle's present proprietor, the Countess Maria Regina, the haughty daughter, the ghost-lady herself, as found on the rainy day in the tower.

"I am so well, so happy, so rich in life and thoughts and hopes! I owe it all to you, and I thank you again and still again, and sign my last letter from the Halden with the sweet salutation of the country, 'Grüss' Gott!'

> "Devotedly yours,
> "MORRIS DAVIDSON.

"*Midnight, June the first.*"

In the same mail Miss Valentine received a letter from her niece and name-sake, who was travelling with friends from Munich to Geneva.

"MY DEAREST AUNT,—I can't possibly go to sleep without telling you about this beautiful day. Of course you knew we were going through Zurich, but you did

not know we were going to give ourselves
the joy of stopping for a little glimpse of
the Halden country.

" We took a very early train this morning, and without waiting at the village,
went directly on that glorious ten-mile
walk to Obstalden, and dined at the inn
' Zum Hirschen.'

" You remember it — there where we
tried to express ourselves once in verse:

" The pasture-lands stretched far overhead,
And blooming pathways heavenward led,
As on the best of the land we fed
    At the pleasant inn ' Zum Hirschen.'

" Above us, a sky of wondrous blue;
Below, a lake of marvellous hue;
And glad seemed life — the whole way
    through,
    That day as we dined ' Zum Hirschen.'

" And that was how life seemed to-day,
but we were wise enough not to attempt
poetry. When we got back to the village
at night, we climbed up to the castle for
supper. I did so hope to see your Mr.
Davidson; unfortunately he had gone
off for a long tramp. You should hear
die alte Grossmutter talk about him;
she can't begin to say flattering things
enough. And where do you think I went,
Aunt Olivia? Into our old room, to be

sure—your Mr. Davidson's room now—the
door was open, and so I entered.

"Oh, the view from that window!—the
snow - tipped mountain over across the
quiet lake, the little village, the castle
garden, with its terraces and bowers! I
wanted you so much!

"Suddenly I had a feeling as if some
one were coming, and very gently I pushed aside the panel door, closed it behind
me, and descended in the dark — not a
minute too soon, as it proved, because,
firstly, when I looked back there was a
light in the room above; and secondly,
the rest of the party had gone to the station, expecting to find me there, and I
arrived just in time to prevent us from
missing the train.

"And, oh, dear Aunt Olivia, your Mr.
Davidson has made some wonderful dis-
covery. Die alte Grossmutter couldn't
resist telling me, although she wouldn't
tell me what it was; she said he was intending to bring it, or them, to you as a
present, and he might be wishing to make
it a surprise, and it wasn't for her to go
and spoil it all. Now what do you suppose it can be? I am consumed with
curiosity, and could shed tears of envy.
He doesn't know a word about the secret
stairway. Die alte Grossmutter hadn't

thought to mention it. Imagine that!
So exactly like people who possess unusual things not to appreciate them.
When you build your house do put in a
secret stairway, they are so convenient.
The castle garden to-day was a perfect
wilderness of roses; we brought as many
as we could back to Zurich, and one I
left on the window-ledge of our old room
—an unsigned offering from a past to a
present occupant. It was a red rose too,
and therefore of particularly good omen
at the Halden. I wonder if your Mr.
Davidson has found it yet, and is asking
himself how it came?

"And now, my dearest Aunt Olivia, I
kiss you good-night, and end my letter
with the sweet salutation which we have
been hearing all day from peasant folk—
'Grüss' Gott!'

"Lovingly, your namesake niece,

"OLIVIA.

"*Midnight, June the first.*"

Perdita

BY HILDEGARDE HAWTHORNE

I.—ALFALFA RANCH

ALFALFA RANCH, low, wide, with spreading verandas all overgrown by roses and woodbine, and commanding on all sides a wide view of the rolling alfalfa-fields, was a most bewitching place for a young couple to spend the first few months of their married life. So Jack and I were naturally much delighted when Aunt Agnes asked us to consider it our own for as long as we chose. The ranch, in spite of its distance from the nearest town, surrounded as it was by the prairies, and without a neighbor within a three-mile radius, was yet luxuriously fitted with all the modern conveniences. Aunt Agnes was a rich young widow, and had built the place after her husband's death, intending to live there with her child, to whom she transferred all the wealth of devotion she had lavished on her husband. The child, however, had died when only three years old, and Aunt Agnes, as soon as she recovered sufficient strength, had left Alfalfa Ranch, intending never to visit the place again. All this had happened nearly ten years ago, and the widow, relinquishing all the advantages her youth and beauty, quite as much as her wealth, could give her, had devoted herself to work amid the poor of New York.

At my wedding, which she heartily approved, and where to a greater extent than ever before she cast off the almost morbid quietness which had grown habitual with her, she seemed particularly anxious that Jack and I should accept the loan of Alfalfa Ranch, apparently having an old idea that the power of our happiness would somehow lift the cloud of sorrow which, in her mind, brooded over the place. I had not been strong, and Jack was overjoyed at such an opportunity of taking me into the country. High as our expectations were, the beauty of the place far exceeded them all. What color! What glorious sunsets! And the long rides we took, seeming to be utterly tireless in that fresh sweet air!

One afternoon I sat on the veranda at the western wing of the house. The ve-

randa here was broader than elsewhere,
and it was reached only by a flight of
steps leading up from the lawn on one
side, and by a door opposite these steps
that opened into Jack's study. The rest
of this veranda was enclosed by a high
railing, and by wire nettings so thickly
overgrown with vines that the place was
always very shady. I sat near the steps,
where I could watch the sweep of the
great shadows thrown by the clouds that
were sailing before the west wind. Jack
was inside, writing, and now and then he
would say something to me through the
open window. As I sat, lost in delight
at the beauty of the view and the sweetness of the flower-scented air, I marvelled
that Aunt Agnes could ever have left so
charming a spot. " She must still love
it," I thought, getting up to move my
chair to where I might see still further
over the prairies, " and some time she will
come back—" At this moment I happened to glance to the further end of the
veranda, and there I saw, to my amazement, a little child seated on the floor,
playing with the shifting shadows of the
tangled creepers. It was a little girl in
a daintily embroidered white dress, with
golden curls around her baby head. As
I still gazed, she suddenly turned, with a

roguish toss of the yellow hair, and fixed her serious blue eyes on me.

"Baby!" I cried. "Where did you come from? Where's your mamma, darling?" And I took a step towards her.

"What's that, Silvia?" called Jack from within. I turned my head and saw him sitting at his desk.

"Come quick, Jack; there's the loveliest baby—" I turned back to the child, looked, blinked, and at this moment Jack stepped out beside me.

"Baby?" he inquired. "What on earth are you talking about, Silvia dearest?"

"Why, but—" I exclaimed. "There *was* one! How did she get away? She was sitting right there when I called."

"A *baby!*" repeated my husband. "My dear, babies don't appear and disappear like East-Indian magicians. You have been napping, and are trying to conceal the shameful fact."

"Jack," I said, decisively, "don't you suppose I know a baby when I see one? She was sitting right there, playing with the shadows, and I— It's certainly very queer!"

Jack grinned. "Go and put on your habit," he replied; "the horses will be here in ten minutes. And remember that when you have accounted for her disap-

pearance, her presence still remains to be
explained. Or perhaps you think Wah
Sing produced her from his sleeve?"

I laughed. Wah Sing was our Chinese
cook, and more apt, I thought, to put
something up his sleeve than to take anything out.

"I suppose I *was* dreaming," I said,
"though I could almost as well believe I
had only dreamed our marriage."

"Or rather," observed Jack, "that our
marriage had only dreamed us."

II.—SHADOWS

About a week later I received a letter
from Aunt Agnes. Among other things,
chiefly relating to New York's slums, she
said:

"I am in need of rest, and if you and
Jack could put up with me for a few days,
I believe I should like to get back to the
old place. As you know, I have always
dreaded a return there, but lately I seem
somehow to have lost that dread. I feel
that the time has come for me to be there
again, and I am sure you will not mind
me."

Most assuredly we would not mind her.
We sat in the moonlight that night on
the veranda, Jack swinging my hammock

slowly, and talked of Aunt Agnes. The moon silvered the waving alfalfa, and sifted through the twisted vines that fenced us in, throwing intricate and ever-changing patterns on the smooth flooring. There was a hum of insects in the air, and the soft wind ever and anon blew a fleecy cloud over the moon, dimming for a moment her serene splendor.

"Who knows?" said Jack, lighting another cigar. "This may be a turning-point in Aunt Agnes's life, and she may once more be something like the sunny, happy girl your mother describes. She is beautiful, and she is yet young. It may mean the beginning of a new life for her."

"Yes," I answered. "It isn't right that her life should always be shadowed by that early sorrow. She is so lovely, and could be so happy. Now that she has taken the first step, there is no reason why she shouldn't go on."

"We'll do what we can to help her," responded my husband. "Let me fix your cushions, darling; they have slipped." He rose to do so, and suddenly stood still, facing the further end of the veranda. His expression was so peculiar that I turned, following the direction of his eyes, even before his smothered excla-

mation of "Silvia, look there!" reached
me.

Standing in the fluttering moonlight
and shadows was the same little girl I
had seen already. She still wore white,
and her tangled curls floated shining
around her head. She seemed to be smiling, and slightly shook her head at us.

"What does it mean, Jack?" I whispered, slipping out of the hammock.

"How did she get there? Come!" said
he, and we walked hastily towards the
little thing, who again shook her head.
Just at this moment another cloud obscured the moon for a few seconds, and
though in the uncertain twilight I fancied
I still saw her, yet when the cloud passed
she was not to be found.

III.—PERDITA

Aunt Agnes certainly did look as
though she needed rest. She seemed
very frail, and the color had entirely left
her face. But her curling hair was as
golden as ever, and her figure as girlish
and graceful. She kissed me tenderly,
and kept my hand in hers as she wandered over the house and took long looks
across the prairie.

"Isn't it beautiful?" she asked, softly.

"Just the place to be happy in! I've always had a strange fancy that I should
be happy here again some day, and now I
feel as though that day had almost come.
You are happy, aren't you, dear?"

I looked at Jack, and felt the tears
coming to my eyes. "Yes, I am happy.
I did not know one could be so happy," I
answered, after a moment.

. Aunt Agnes smiled her sweet smile
and kissed me again. "God bless you
and your Jack! You almost make me
feel young again."

"As though you could possibly feel
anything else," I retorted, laughing.
"You little humbug, to pretend you are
old!" and slipping my arm round her
waist, for we had always been dear
friends, I walked off to chat with her in
her room.

We took a ride that afternoon, for
Aunt Agnes wanted another gallop over
that glorious prairie. The exercise and
the perfect afternoon brought back the
color to her cheeks.

"I think I shall be much better to-
morrow," she observed, as we trotted
home. "What a country this is, and
what horses!" slipping her hand down
her mount's glossy neck. "I did right
to come back here. I do not believe I

will go away again." And she smiled on
Jack and me, who laughed, and said she
would find it a difficult thing to attempt.

We all three came out on the veranda
to see the sunset. It was always a glorious sight, but this evening it was more
than usually magnificent. Immense rays
of pale blue and pink spread over the sky,
and the clouds, which stretched in hori-
zontal masses, glowed rose and golden.
The whole sky was luminous and tender,
and seemed to tremble with light.

We sat silent, looking at the sky and
at the shadowy grass that seemed to meet
it. Slowly the color deepened and faded.

"There can never be a lovelier evening," said Aunt Agnes, with a sigh.

"Don't say that," replied Jack. "It is
only the beginning of even more perfect
ones."

Aunt Agnes rose with a slight shiver,
"It grows chilly when the sun goes,"
she murmured, and turned lingeringly to
enter the house. Suddenly she gave a
startled exclamation. Jack and I jumped
up and looked at her. She stood with
both hands pressed to her heart, looking—

"The child again," said Jack, in a low
voice, laying his hand on my arm.

He was right. There in the gathering
shadow stood the little girl in the white

dress. Her hands were stretched towards
us, and her lips parted in a smile. A be-
lated gleam of sunlight seemed to linger
in her hair.

"Perdita!" cried Aunt Agnes, in a
voice that shook with a kind of terrible
joy. Then, with a stifled sob, she ran
forward and sank before the baby, throwing her arms about her. The little girl
leaned back her golden head and looked
at Aunt Agnes with her great, serious
eyes. Then she flung both baby arms
round her neck, and lifted her sweet
mouth—

Jack and I turned away, looking at
each other with tears in our eyes. A
slight sound made us turn back. Aunt
Agnes had fallen forward to the floor,
and the child was nowhere to be seen.

We rushed up, and Jack raised my
aunt in his arms and carried her into
the house. But she was quite dead. The
little child we never saw again.

At La Glorieuse

BY M. E. M. DAVIS

MADAME RAYMONDE-AR-
NAULT leaned her head against
the back of her garden chair, and
watched the young people furtively
from beneath her half-closed eyelids.
"He is about to speak," she murmured
under her breath; "she, at least, will be
happy!" and her heart fluttered violently, as if it had been her own thin blood-
less hand which Richard Keith was holding in his; her dark sunken eyes, instead of Félice's brown ones, which
drooped beneath his tender gaze.

Marcelite, the old *bonne,* who stood
erect and stately behind her mistress,
permitted herself also to regard them
for a moment with something like a
smile relaxing her sombre yellow face;
then she too turned her turbaned head
discreetly in another direction.

The plantation house at La Glorieuse
is built in a shining loop of Bayou L'Epe-

12   S. H. D.

ron. A level grassy lawn, shaded by
enormous live-oaks, stretches across from
the broad stone steps to the sodded levee,
where a flotilla of small boats, drawn up
among the flags and lily-pads, rise and
fall with the lapping waves. On the left
of the house the white cabins of the quarter show their low roofs above the shrub-
bery; to the right the plantations of cane,
following the inward curve of the bayou,
sweep southward field after field, their
billowy blue-green reaches blending far
in the rear with the indistinct purple
haze of the swamp. The great square
house, raised high on massive stone pil-
lars, dates back to the first quarter of the
century; its sloping roof is set with rows
of dormer-windows, the big red double
chimneys rising oddly from their midst;
wide galleries with fluted columns en-
close it on three sides; from the fourth
is projected a long narrow wing, two
stories in height, which stands somewhat
apart from the main building, but is connected with it by a roofed and latticed
passageway. The lower rooms of this
wing open upon small porticos, with bal-
ustrades of wrought ironwork rarely fanciful and delicate. From these you may
step into the rose garden — a tangled
pleasaunce which rambles away through

alleys of wild-peach and magnolia to an
orange grove, whose trees are gnarled
and knotted with the growth of half a
century.

The early shadows were cool and dewy
there that morning; the breath of damask-roses was sweet on the air; brown,
gold - dusted butterflies were hovering
over the sweet - pease abloom in sunny
corners; birds shot up now and then from
the leafy aisles, singing, into the clear
blue sky above; the chorus of the negroes
at work among the young cane floated in,
mellow and resonant, from the fields.
The old mistress of La Glorieuse saw it
all behind her drooped eyelids. Was it
not April too, that long-gone unforgot-
ten morning? And were not the bees
busy in the hearts of the roses, and the
birds singing, when Richard Keith, the
first of the name who came to La Glorieuse, held her hand in his, and whispered
his love - story yonder, by the ragged
thicket of crêpe - myrtle? Ah, Félice,
my child, thou art young, but I too have
had my sixteen years; and yellow as are
the curls on the head bent over thine,
those of the first Richard were more
golden still. And the second Richard, he
who—

Marcelite's hand fell heavily on her

mistress's shoulder. Madame Arnault
opened her eyes and sat up, grasping the
arms of her chair. A harsh grating
sound had fallen suddenly into the stillness, and the shutters of one of the upper
windows of the wing which overlooked
the garden were swinging slowly out-
ward. A ripple of laughter, musical and
mocking, rang clearly on the air; at the
same moment a woman appeared, framed
like a portrait in the narrow casement.
She crossed her arms on the iron window-
bar, and gazed silently down on the
startled group below. She was strangely beautiful and young, though an air of
soft and subtle maturity pervaded her
graceful figure. A glory of yellow hair
encircled her pale oval face, and waved
away in fluffy masses to her waist; her
full lips were scarlet; her eyes, beneath
their straight dark brows, were gray, with
emerald shadows in their luminous
depths. Her low-cut gown, of some thin,
yellowish-white material, exposed her exquisitely rounded throat and perfect
neck; long, flowing sleeves of spidery
lace fell away from her shapely arms,
leaving them bare to the shoulder; loose
strings of pearls were wound around her
small wrists, and about her throat was
clasped a strand of blood-red coral, from

which hung to the hollow of her bosom
a single translucent drop of amber. A
smile at once daring and derisive parted
her lips; an elusive light came and went
in her eyes.

Keith had started impatiently from his
seat at the unwelcome interruption. He
stood regarding the intruder with mute,
half-frowning inquiry.

Félice turned a bewildered face to her
grandmother. "Who is it, mère?" she
whispered. "Did — did you give her
leave?"

Madame Arnault had sunk back in her
chair. Her hands trembled convulsively
still, and the lace on her bosom rose and
fell with the hurried beating of her heart.
But she spoke in her ordinary measured,
almost formal tones, as she put out a
hand and drew the girl to her side. "I
do not know, my child. Perhaps Suzette
Beauvais has come over with her guests
from Grandchamp. I thought I heard
but now the sound of boats on the bayou.
Suzette is ever ready with her pranks.
Or perhaps—"

She stopped abruptly. The stranger
was drawing the batten blinds together.
Her ivory-white arms gleamed in the sun.
For a moment they could see her face
shining like a star against the dusky

glooms within; then the bolt was shot sharply to its place.

Old Marcelite drew a long breath of relief as she disappeared. A smothered ejaculation had escaped her lips, under the girl's intent gaze; an ashen gray had overspread her dark face. "Mam'selle Suzette, she been an' dress up one o' her young ladies jes fer er trick," she said, slowly, wiping the great drops of perspiration from her wrinkled forehead.

"Suzette?" echoed Félice, incredulously. "She would never dare! Who *can* it be?"

"It is easy enough to find out," laughed Keith. "Let us go and see for ourselves who is masquerading in my quarters."

He drew her with him as he spoke along the winding violet-bordered walks which led to the house. She looked anxiously back over her shoulder at her grandmother. Madame Arnault half arose, and made an imperious gesture of dissent; but Marcelite forced her gently into her seat, and leaning forward, whispered a few words rapidly in her ear.

"Thou art right, Marcelite," she acquiesced, with a heavy sigh. "'Tis better so."

They spoke in *nègre,* that mysterious

patois which is so uncouth in itself, so
soft and caressing on the lips of women.
Madame Arnault signed to the girl to go
on. She shivered a little, watching their
retreating figures. The old *bonne* threw
a light shawl about her shoulders, and
crouched affectionately at her feet. The
murmur of their voices as they talked
long and earnestly together hardly reached beyond the shadows of the wild-peach-
tree beneath which they sat.

"How beautiful she was!" Félice said,
musingly, as they approached the latticed
passageway.

"Well, yes," her companion returned,
carelessly. "I confess I do not greatly
fancy that style of beauty myself." And
he glanced significantly down at her own
flower-like face.

She flushed, and her brown eyes drooped, but a bright little smile played about
her sensitive mouth. "I cannot see," she
declared, "how Suzette could have dared
to take her friends into the ballroom!"

"Why?" he asked, smiling at her vehe-
mence.

She stopped short in her surprise. "Do
you not know, then?" She sank her
voice to a whisper. "The ballroom has
never been opened since the night my
mother died. I was but a baby then,

though sometimes I imagine that I remember it all. There was a grand ball
there that night. La Glorieuse was full
of guests, and everybody from all the
plantations around was here. Mère has
never told me how it was, nor Marcelite;
but the other servants used to talk to me
about my beautiful young mother, and
tell me how she died suddenly in her ball
dress, while the ball was going on. My
father had the whole wing closed at once,
and no one was ever allowed to enter it.
I used to be afraid to play in its shadow,
and if I did stray anywhere near it, my
father would always call me away. Her
death must have broken his heart. He
rarely spoke; I never saw him smile; and
his eyes were so sad that I could weep
now at remembering them. Then he
too died while I was still a little girl, and
now I have no one in the world but dear
old mère." Her voice trembled a little,
but she flushed, and smiled again beneath
his meaning look. "It was many years
before even the lower floor was reopened,
and I am almost sure that yours is the
only room there which has ever been
used."

They stepped, as she concluded, into the
hall.

"I have never been in here before," she

said, looking about her with shy curiosity. A flood of sunlight poured through
the wide arched window at the foot of the
stair. The door of the room nearest the
entrance stood open; the others, ranging
along the narrow hall, were all closed.

"This is my room," he said, nodding
towards the open door.

She turned her head quickly away,
with an impulse of girlish modesty, and
ran lightly up the stair. He glanced
downward as he followed, and paused,
surprised to see the flutter of white garments in a shaded corner of his room.
Looking more closely, he saw that it was
a glimmer of light from an open window
on the dark polished floor.

The upper hall was filled with sombre
shadows; the motionless air was heavy
with a musty, choking odor. In the dimness a few tattered hangings were visible
on the walls; a rope, with bits of crumbling evergreen clinging to it, trailed
from above one of the low windows. The
panelled double door of the ballroom
was shut; no sound came from behind it.

"The girls have seen us coming," said
Félice, picking her way daintily across
the dust-covered floor, "and they have
hidden themselves inside."

Keith pushed open the heavy valves,

which creaked noisily on their rusty
hinges. The gloom within was murkier
still; the chill dampness, with its smell
of mildew and mould, was like that of a
funeral vault.

The large, low-ceilinged room ran the
entire length of the house. A raised dais,
whose faded carpet had half rotted away,
occupied an alcove at one end; upon it
four or five wooden stools were placed;
one of these was overturned; on another
a violin in its baggy green baize cover
was lying. Straight high-backed chairs
were pushed against the walls on either
side; in front of an open fireplace was a
low wooden mantel two small cushioned
divans were drawn up, with a claw-footed
table between them. A silver salver filled
with tall glasses was set carelessly on one
edge of the table; a half-open fan of
sandal-wood lay beside it; a man's glove
had fallen on the hearth just within
the tarnished brass fender. Cobwebs de-
pended from the ceiling, and hung in
loose threads from the mantel; dust was
upon everything, thick and motionless; a
single ghostly ray of light that filtered in
through a crevice in one of the shutters
was weighted with gray lustreless motes.
The room was empty and silent. The
visitors, who had come so stealthily, had

as stealthily departed, leaving no trace
behind them.

"They have played us a pretty trick,"
said Keith, gayly. "They must have fled
as soon as they saw us start towards the
house." He went over to the window
from which the girl had looked down
into the rose garden, and gave it a shake.
The dust flew up in a suffocating cloud,
and the spiked nails which secured the
upper sash rattled in their places.

"That is like Suzette Beauvais," Félice
replied, absently. She was not thinking
of Suzette. She had forgotten even the
stranger, whose disdainful eyes, fixed
upon herself, had moved her sweet nature
to something like a rebellious anger. Her
thoughts were on the beautiful young
mother of alien race, whose name, for
some reason, she was forbidden to speak.
She saw her glide, gracious and smiling,
along the smooth floor; she heard her
voice above the call and response of the
violins; she breathed the perfume of her
laces, backward-blown by the swift motion of the dance!

She strayed dreamily about, touching
with an almost reverent finger first one
worm-eaten object and then another, as
if by so doing he could make the imagined scene more real. Her eyes were

downcast; the blood beneath her rich
dark skin came and went in brilliant
flushes on her cheeks; the bronze hair,
piled in heavy coils on her small, well-
poised head, fell in loose rings on her
low forehead and against her white neck;
her soft gray gown, following the harmo-
nious lines of her slender figure, seemed
to envelop her like a twilight cloud.

"She is adorable," said Richard Keith
to himself.

It was the first time that he had been
really alone with her, though this was
the third week of his stay in the hospita-
ble old mansion where his father and
his grandfather before him had been welcome guests. Now that he came to think
of it, in that bundle of yellow, time-worn
letters from Félix Arnault to Richard
Keith, which he had found among his
father's papers, was one which described
at length a ball in this very ballroom.
Was it in celebration of his marriage, or
of his home-coming after a tour abroad?
Richard could not remember. But he
idly recalled portions of other letters, as
he stood with his elbow on the mantel
watching Félix Arnault's daughter.

"*Your son and my daughter,*" the
phrase which had made him smile when
he read it yonder in his Maryland home,

brought now a warm glow to his heart.
The half-spoken avowal, the question that
had trembled on his lips a few moments
ago in the rose garden, stirred impetu-
ously within him.

Félice stepped down from the dais
where she had been standing, and came
swiftly across the room, as if his unspo-
ken thought had called her to him. A
tender rapture possessed him to see her
thus drawing towards him; he longed to
stretch out his arms and fold her to his
breast. He moved, and his hand came in
contact with a small object on the mantel. He picked it up. It was a ring, a
band of dull worn gold, with a confused
tracery graven upon it. He merely
glanced at it, slipping it mechanically on
his finger. His eyes were full upon hers,
which were suffused and shining.

"Did you speak?" she asked, timidly.
She had stopped abruptly, and was looking at him with a hesitating, half-bewil-
dered expression.

"No," he replied. His mood had
changed. He walked again to the window and examined the clumsy bolt.
"Strange!" he muttered. "I have never
seen a face like hers," he sighed, dreamily.

"She was very beautiful," Félice returned, quietly. "I think we must be going," she added. "Mère will be growing impatient." The flush had died out of her cheek, her arms hung listlessly at her side. She shuddered as she gave a last look around the desolate room. "They were dancing here when my mother died," she said to herself.

He preceded her slowly down the stair. The remembrance of the woman began vaguely to stir his senses. He had hardly remarked her then, absorbed as he had been in another idea. Now she seemed to swim voluptuously before his vision; her tantalizing laugh rang in his ears; her pale perfumed hair was blown across his face; he felt its filmy strands upon his lips and eyelids. "Do you think," he asked, turning eagerly on the bottom step, "that they could have gone into any of these rooms?"

She shrank unaccountably from him. "Oh no," she cried. "They are in the rose garden with mère, or they have gone around to the lawn. Come"; and she hurried out before him.

Madame Arnault looked at them sharply as they came up to where she was sitting. "No one!" she echoed, in response to Keith's report. "Then they really have gone back?"

"Madame knows dat we is hear de boats pass up de bayou whilse m'sieu an' mam'selle was inside," interposed Marcelite, stooping to pick up her mistress's cane.

"I would not have thought Suzette so —so indiscreet," said Félice. There was a note of weariness in her voice.

Madame Arnault looked anxiously at her and then at Keith. The young man was staring abstractedly at the window, striving to recall the vision that had appeared there, and he felt, rather than saw, his hostess start and change color when her eyes fell upon the ring he was wearing. He lifted his hand covertly, and turned the trinket around in the light, but he tried in vain to decipher the irregular characters traced upon it.

"Let us go in," said the old madame. "Félice, my child, thou art fatigued."

Now when in all her life before was Félice ever fatigued? Félice, whose strong young arms could send a pirogue flying up the bayou for miles; Félice, who was ever ready for a tramp along the rose-hedged lanes to the swamp lakes when the water-lilies were in bloom; to the sugar-house in grinding-time, down the levee road to St. Joseph's, the little brown ivy-grown church, whose solitary spire

arose slim and straight above the encir-
cling trees.

Marcelite gave an arm to her mistress,
though, in truth, she seemed to walk a little unsteadily herself. Félice followed
with Keith, who was silent and self-ab-
sorbed.

The day passed slowly, a constraint had
somehow fallen upon the little household.
Madame Arnault's fine high-bred old face
wore its customary look of calm repose,
but her eyes now and then sought her
guest with an expression which he could
not have fathomed if he had observed it.
But he saw nothing. A mocking red
mouth; a throat made for the kisses of
love; white arms strung with pearls—
these were ever before him, shutting away
even the pure sweet face of Félice
Arnault.

"Why did I not look at her more
closely when I had the opportunity, fool
that I was?" he asked himself, savagely,
again and again, revolving in his mind a
dozen pretexts for going at once to the
Beauvais plantation, a mile or so up the
bayou. But he felt an inexplicable shy-
ness at the thought of putting any of
these plans into action, and so allowed the
day to drift by. He arose gladly when
the hour for retiring came — that hour

which he had hitherto postponed by every
means in his power. He kissed, as usual,
the hand of his hostess, and held that of
Félice in his for a moment; but he did
not feel its trembling, or see the timid
trouble in her soft eyes.

His room in the silent and deserted
wing was full of fantastic shadows. He
threw himself on a chair beside a window
without lighting his lamp. The rose garden outside was steeped in moonlight; the
magnolia bells gleamed waxen - white
against their glossy green leaves; the
vines on the tall trellises threw a soft
network of dancing shadows on the white-
shelled walks below; the night air stealing about was loaded with the perfume
of roses and sweet-olive; a mocking-bird
sang in an orange-tree, his mate respond-
ing sleepily from her nest in the old
summer-house.

"To - morrow," he murmured, half
aloud, "I will go to Grandchamp and
give her the ring she left in the old ballroom."

He looked at it glowing dully in the
moonlight; suddenly he lifted his head,
listening. Did a door grind somewhere
near on its hinges? He got up cautiously and looked out. It was not fancy. She was standing full in view on

13 S. H. D.

the small balcony of the room next his
own. Her white robes waved to and fro
in the breeze; the pearls on her arms glis-
tened. Her face, framed in the pale gold
of her hair, was turned towards him; a
smile curved her lips; her mysterious
eyes seemed to be searching his through
the shadow. He drew back, confused
and trembling, and when, a second later,
he looked again, she was gone.

He sat far into the night, his brain
whirling, his blood on fire. Who was
she, and what was the mystery hidden in
this isolated old plantation house? His
thoughts reverted to the scene in the
rose garden, and he went over and over
all its details. He remembered Madame
Arnault's agitation when the window
opened and the girl appeared; her evident
discomfiture — of which at the time he
had taken no heed, but which came back
to him vividly enough now—at his pro-
posal to visit the ballroom; her startled
recognition of the ring on his finger; her
slurring suggestion of visitors from
Grandchamp; the look of terror on Marcelite's face. What did it all mean? Félice,
he was sure, knew nothing. But here, in
an unused portion of the house, which
even the members of the family had never
visited, a young and beautiful girl was

shut up a prisoner, condemned perhaps to a life-long captivity.

"Good God!" He leaped to his feet at the thought. He would go and thunder at Madame Arnault's door, and demand an explanation. But no; not yet. He calmed himself with an effort. By too great haste he might injure her. "Insane?" He laughed aloud at the idea of madness in connection with that exquisite creature.

It dawned upon him, as he paced restlessly back and forth, that although his father had been here more than once in his youth and manhood, he had never heard him speak of La Glorieuse nor of Félix Arnault, whose letters he had read after his father's death a few months ago —those old letters whose affectionate warmth indeed had determined him, in the first desolation of his loss, to seek the family which seemed to have been so bound to his own. Morose and taciturn as his father had been, surely he would sometimes have spoken of his old friend if— Worn out at last with conjecture; beaten back, bruised and breathless, from an enigma which he could not solve; exhausted by listening with strained attention for some movement in the next room, he threw himself on his bed, dressed as he

was, and fell into a heavy sleep, which
lasted far into the forenoon of the next
day.

When he came out (walking like one
in a dream), he found a gay party assembled on the lawn in front of the house.
Suzette Beauvais and her guests, a bevy
of girls, had come from Grandchamp.
They had been joined, as they rowed down
the bayou, by the young people from the
plantation houses on the way. Half a
dozen boats, their long paddles laid across
the seats, were added to the home fleet at
the landing. Their stalwart black rowers were basking in the sun on the levee,
or lounging about the quarter. At the
moment of his appearance, Suzette herself was indignantly disclaiming any
complicity in the jest of the day before.

"Myself, I was making o'ange-flower
conserve," she declared; "an' anyhow I
wouldn't go in that ballroom unless
madame send me."

"But who was it, then?" insisted Félice.

Mademoiselle Beauvais spread out her
fat little hands and lifted her shoulders.
"*Mo pas connais,*" she laughed, dropping
into patois.

Madame Arnault here interposed. It
was but the foolish conceit of some teas-

ing neighbor, she said, and not worth
further discussion. Keith's blood boiled
in his veins at this calm dismissal of the
subject, but he gave no sign. He saw her
glance warily at himself from time to
time.

"I will sift the matter to the bottom,"
he thought, "and I will force her to confess the truth, whatever it may be, before
the world."

The noisy chatter and meaningless
laughter around him jarred upon his
nerves; he longed to be alone with his
thoughts; and presently, pleading a head-
ache—indeed his temples throbbed almost
to bursting, and his eyes were hot and
dry—he quitted the lawn, seeing but not
noting until long afterwards, when they
smote his memory like a two-edged knife,
the pain in Félice's uplifted eyes, and the
little sorrowful quiver of her mouth. He
strolled around the corner of the house to
his apartment. The blinds of the arched
window were drawn, and a hazy twilight
was diffused about the hall, though it was
mid-afternoon outside. As he entered,
closing the door behind him, the woman
at that moment uppermost in his thoughts
came down the dusky silence from the
further end of the hall. She turned her
inscrutable eyes upon him in passing,

and flitted noiselessly and with languid grace up the stairway, the faint swish of her gown vanishing with her. He hesitated a moment, overpowered by conflicting emotion; then he sprang recklessly after her.

He pushed open the ballroom door, reaching his arms out blindly before him. Once more the great dust-covered room was empty. He strained his eyes helplessly into the obscurity. A chill reaction passed over him; he felt himself on the verge of a swoon. He did not this time even try to discover the secret door or exit by which she had disappeared; he looked, with a hopeless sense of discouragement, at the barred windows, and turned to leave the room. As he did so, he saw a handkerchief lying on the threshold of the door. He picked it up eagerly, and pressed it to his lips. A peculiar delicate perfume which thrilled his senses lurked in its gossamer folds. As he was about thrusting it into his breast-pocket, he noticed in one corner a small blood-stain fresh and wet. He had then bitten his lip in his excitement.

"I need no further proof," he said aloud, and his own voice startled him, echoing down the long hall. "She is beyond all question a prisoner in this

detached building, which has mysterious
exits and entrances. She has been forced
to promise that she will not go outside
of its walls, or she is afraid to do so. I
will bring home this monstrous crime.
I will release this lovely young woman
who dares not speak, yet so plainly ap-
peals to me." Already he saw in fancy
her starlike eyes raised to his in mute
gratitude, her white hand laid confid-
ingly on his arm.

The party of visitors remained at La
Glorieuse overnight. The negro fiddlers
came in, and there was dancing in the
old-fashioned double parlors and on the
moonlit galleries. Félice was unnatu-
rally gay. Keith looked on gloomily,
taking no part in the amusement.

"*Il est bien bête,* your yellow-haired
Marylander," whispered Suzette Beauvais to her friend.

He went early to his room, but he
watched in vain for some sign from his
beautiful neighbor. He grew sick with
apprehension. Had Madame Arnault—
But no; she would not dare. "I will
wait one more day," he finally decided;
" and then—"

The next morning, after a late breakfast, some one proposed impromptu cha-
rades and tableaux. Madame Arnault

good-naturedly sent for the keys to the
tall presses built into the walls, which
contained the accumulated trash and
treasure of several generations. Mounted on a stepladder, Robert Beauvais ex-
plored the recesses, and threw down to
the laughing crowd embroidered shawls
and scarfs yellow with age, soft muslins
of antique pattern, stiff big-flowered
brocades, scraps of gauze ribbon, gossamer laces. On one topmost shelf he
came upon a small wooden box inlaid
with mother-of-pearl. Félice reached up
for it, and, moved by some undefined
impulse, Richard came and stood by her
side while she opened it. A perfume
which he recognized arose from it as she
lifted a fold of tissue-paper. Some
strings of Oriental pearls of extraordinary size, and perfect in shape and color,
were coiled underneath, with a coral
necklace, whose pendant of amber had
broken off and rolled into a corner.
With them—he hardly restrained an exclamation, and his hand involuntarily
sought his breast-pocket at sight of the
handkerchief with a drop of fresh blood
in one corner! Félice trembled without
knowing why. Madame Arnault, who
had just entered the room, took the box
from her quietly, and closed the lid with

a snap. The girl, accustomed to implicit obedience, asked no questions; the others, engaged in turning over the old-time finery, had paid no attention.

"Does she think to disarm me by such puerile tricks?" he thought, turning a look of angry warning on the old madame; and in the steady gaze which she fixed on him he read a haughty defiance.

He forced himself to enter into the sports of the day, and he walked down to the boat-landing a little before sunset to see the guests depart. As the line of boats swept away, the black rowers dipping their oars lightly in the placid waves, he turned with a sense of release, leaving Madame Arnault and Félice still at the landing, and went down the levee road towards St. Joseph's. The field gang, whose red, blue, and brown blouses splotched the squares of cane with color, was preparing to quit work; loud laughter and noisy jests rang out on the air; high-wheeled plantation wagons creaked along the lanes; negro children, with dip-nets and fishing-poles over their shoulders, ran homeward along the levee, the dogs at their heels barking joyously; a schooner, with white sail outspread, was stealing like a fairy bark around a distant bend of the

bayou; the silvery waters were turning
to gold under a sunset sky.

It was twilight when he struck across
the plantation, and came around by the
edge of the swamp to the clump of trees
in a corner of the home field which he
had often remarked from his window.
As he approached, he saw a woman come
out of the dense shadow, as if intending
to meet him, and then draw back again.
His heart throbbed painfully, but he
walked steadily forward. It was only
Félice. *Only Félice!* She was sitting
on a flat tombstone. The little spot was
the Raymonde-Arnault family burying-
ground. There were many marble head-
stones and shafts, and two broad low
tombs side by side and a little apart
from the others. A tangle of rose-briers
covered the sunken graves, a rank growth
of grass choked the narrow paths, the
little gate interlaced and overhung with
honeysuckle sagged away from its posts,
the fence itself had lost a picket here
and there, and weeds flaunted boldly in
the gaps. The girl looked wan and
ghostly in the lonely dusk.

"This is my father's grave, and my
mother is here," she said, abruptly, as
he came up and stood beside her. Her
head was drooped upon her breast, and

he saw that she had been weeping.
"See," she went on, drawing her finger
along the mildewed lettering: "'Félix Marie-Joseph Arnault ... âgé de
trente-quatre ans' ... 'Hélène Pallacier, épouse de Félix Arnault ... dé-
cédée à l'âge de dix-neuf ans.' Nine-
teen years old," she repeated, slowly.
"My mother was one year younger than
I am when she died — my beautiful
mother!"

Her voice sounded like a far-away
murmur in his ears. He looked at her,
vaguely conscious that she was suffering.
But he did not speak, and after a little
she got up and went away. Her dress,
which brushed him in passing, was wet
with dew. He watched her slight figure,
moving like a spirit along the lane, until
a turn in the hedge hid her from sight.
Then he turned again towards the
swamp, and resumed his restless walk.

Some hours later he crossed the rose
garden. The moon was under a cloud;
the trunks of the crêpe-myrtles were like
pale spectres in the uncertain light. The
night wind blew in chill and moist from
the swamp. The house was dark and
quiet, but he heard the blind of an upper
window turned stealthily as he stepped
into the latticed arcade.

"The old madame is watching me—
and her," he said to himself.

His agitation had now become supreme. The faint familiar perfume that
stole about his room filled him with a
kind of frenzy. Was this the chivalric
devotion of which he had so boasted?
this the desire to protect a young and
defenceless woman? He no longer dared
question himself. He seemed to feel her
warm breath against his cheeks. He
threw up his arms with a gesture of despair. A sigh stirred the deathlike stillness. At last! She was there, just
within his doorway; the pale glimmer of
the veiled moon fell upon her. Her
trailing laces wrapped her about like a
silver mist; her arms were folded across
her bosom; her eyes—he dared not interpret the meaning which he read in
those wonderful eyes. She turned slowly and went down the hall. He followed
her, reeling like a drunkard. His feet
seemed clogged, the blood ran thick in
his veins, a strange roaring was in his
ears. His hot eyes strained after her as
she vanished, just beyond his touch, into
the room next his own. He threw himself against the closed door in a transport
of rage. It yielded suddenly, as if opened from within. A full blaze of light

struck his eyes, blinding him for an instant; then he saw her. A huge four-
posted bed with silken hangings occupied
a recess in the room. Across its foot a
low couch was drawn. She had thrown
herself there. Her head was pillowed on
crimson gold-embroidered cushions; her
diaphanous draperies, billowing foamlike
over her, half concealed, half revealed her
lovely form; her hair waved away from
her brows, and spread like a shower of
gold over the cushions. One bare arm
hung to the floor; something jewel-like
gleamed in the half-closed hand; the other lay across her forehead, and from beneath it her eyes were fixed upon him.
He sprang forward with a cry. . . .

At first he could remember nothing.
The windows were open; the heavy curtains which shaded them moved lazily in
the breeze; a shaft of sunlight that came
in between them fell upon the polished
surface of the marble mantel. He examined with languid curiosity some trifles
that stood there—a pair of Dresden figures, a blue Sèvres vase of graceful shape,
a bronze clock with gilded rose-wreathed
Cupids; and then raised his eyes to the
two portraits which hung above. One of
these was familiar enough—the dark melancholy face of Félix Arnault, whose por-

trait by different hands and at different
periods of his life hung in nearly every
room of La Glorieuse. The blood surged
into his face and receded again at sight
of the other. Oh, so strangely like! The
yellow hair, the slumberous eyes, the full
throat clasped about with a single strand
of coral. Yes, it was she! He lifted himself on his elbow. He was in bed. Surely this was the room into which she had
drawn him with her eyes. Did he sink
on the threshold, all his senses swooning
into delicious faith? Or had he, indeed,
in that last moment thrown himself on
his knees by her couch? He could not
remember, and he sank back with a sigh.

Instantly Madame Arnault was bending over him. Her cool hands were on his
forehead. *"Dieu merci!"* she exclaimed,
"thou art thyself once more, *mon fils.*"

He seized her hand imperiously. "Tell
me, madame," he demanded—"tell me,
for the love of God! What is she? Who
is she? Why have you shut her away in
this deserted place? Why—"

She was looking down at him with an
expression half of pity, half of pain.

"Forgive me," he faltered, involuntarily, all his darker suspicions somehow
vanishing; "but—oh, tell me!"

"Calm thyself, Richard," she said,

soothingly, seating herself on the side of
the bed, and stroking his hand gently.
Too agitated to speak, he continued to
gaze at her with imploring eyes. "Yes,
yes, I will relate the whole story," she
added, hastily, for he was panting and
struggling for speech. "I heard you fall
last night," she continued, relapsing for
greater ease into French; "for I was full
of anxiety about you, and I lingered long
at my window watching for you. I came
at once with Marcelite, and found you
lying insensible across the threshold of
this room. We lifted you to the bed, and
bled you after the old fashion, and then I
gave you a tisane of my own making,
which threw you into a quiet sleep. I
have watched beside you until your waking. Now you are but a little weak from
fasting and excitement, and when you
have rested and eaten—"

"No," he pleaded; "now, at once!"

"Very well," she said, simply. She was
silent a moment, as if arranging her
thoughts. "Your grandfather, a Richard
Keith like yourself," she began, "was a
collegiate-mate and friend of my brother,
Henri Raymonde, and accompanied him
to La Glorieuse during one of their vaca-
tions. I was already betrothed to Mon-
sieur Arnault, but I— No matter! I

never saw Richard Keith afterwards. But years later he sent your father, who also bore his name, to visit me here. My son, Félix, was but a year or so younger than his boy, and the two lads became at once warm friends. They went abroad, and pursued their studies side by side, like brothers. They came home together, and when Richard's father died, Félix spent nearly a year with him on his Maryland plantation. They exchanged, when apart, almost daily letters. Richard's marriage, which occurred soon after they left college, strengthened rather than weakened this extraordinary bond between them. Then came on the war. They were in the same command, and hardly lost sight of each other during their four years of service.

" When the war was ended, your father went back to his estates. Félix turned his face homeward, but drifted by some strange chance down to Florida, where he met *her* "—she glanced at the portrait over the mantel. " Hélène Pallacier was Greek by descent, her family having been among those brought over some time during the last century as colonists to Florida from the Greek islands. He married her, barely delaying his marriage long enough to write me that he was bringing home a

bride. She was young, hardly more than
a child, indeed, and marvellously beautiful "—Keith moved impatiently; he found
these family details tedious and uninter-
esting — " a radiant soulless creature,
whose only law was her own selfish en-
joyment, and whose coming brought pain
and bitterness to La Glorieuse. These
were her rooms. She chose them because
of the rose garden, for she had a sensuous
and passionate love of nature. She used
to lie for hours on the grass there, with
her arms flung over her head, gazing
dreamily on the fluttering leaves above
her. The pearls—which she always wore
—some coral ornaments, and a handful
of amber beads were her only dower, but
her caprices were the insolent and ex-
travagant caprices of a queen. Félix,
who adored her, gratified them at whatever expense; and I think at first she had
a careless sort of regard for him. But
she hated the little Félice, whose coming
gave her the first pang of physical pain
she had ever known. She never offered
the child a caress. She sometimes looked
at her with a suppressed rage which filled
me with terror and anxiety.

When Félice was a little more than a
year old, your father came to La Glorieuse to pay us a long-promised visit.

His wife had died some months before, and you, a child of six or seven years, were left in charge of relatives in Maryland. Richard was in the full vigor of manhood, broad-shouldered, tall, blue-eyed, and blond-haired, like his father and like you. From the moment of their first meeting Hélène exerted all the power of her fascination to draw him to her. Never had she been so whimsical, so imperious, so bewitching! Loyal to his friend, faithful to his own high sense of honor, he struggled against a growing weakness, and finally fled. I will never forget the night he went away. A ball had been planned by Félix in honor of his friend. The ballroom was decorated under his own supervision. The house was filled with guests from adjoining parishes; everybody, young and old, came from the plantations around. Hélène was dazzling that night. The light of triumph in her cheeks; her eyes shone with a softness which I had never seen in them before. I watched her walking up and down the room with Richard, or floating with him in the dance. They were like a pair of radiant godlike visitants from another world. My heart ached for them in spite of my indignation and apprehension; for light whispers were beginning to circulate, and I saw more than one meaning smile directed at them. Félix, who was truth itself, was gayly unconscious.

"Towards midnight I heard far up the bayou the shrill whistle of the little packet which passed up and down then, as now, twice a week; and presently she swung up to our landing. Richard was standing with Hélène by the fireplace. They had been talking for some time in low earnest tones. A sudden look of determination came into his eyes. I saw him draw from his finger a ring which she had one day playfully bade him wear, and offer it to her. His face was white and strained; hers wore a look which I could not fathom. He quitted her side abruptly, and walked rapidly across the room, threading his way among the dancers, and disappeared in the press about the door. A few moments later a note was handed me. I heard the boat steam away from the landing as I read it. It was a hurried line from Richard. He said that he had been called away on urgent business, and he begged me to make his adieux to Madame Arnault and Félix. Félix was worried and perplexed by the sudden departure of his guest. Hélène said not a word, but very soon I saw her slipping down the stair, and I knew that she had gone to her room. Her absence was not remarked, for the ball was at its height. It was almost daylight when the last dance was concluded, and the guests who were staying in the house had retired to their rooms.

"Félix, having seen to the comfort of all, went at last to join his wife. He burst into my room a second later almost crazed with horror and grief. I followed him to this room. She was lying on a couch at the foot of the bed. One arm was thrown across her forehead, the other hung to the floor, and in her hand she held a tiny silver bottle with a jewelled stopper. A handkerchief, with a single drop of blood upon it, was lying on her bosom. A faint curious odor exhaled from her lips and hung about the room, but the poison had left no other trace.

"No one save ourselves and Marcelite ever knew the truth. She had danced too much at the ball that night, and she had died suddenly of heart-disease. We buried her out yonder in the old Raymonde-Arnault burying-ground. I do not know what the letter contained which Félix wrote to Richard. He never uttered his name afterwards. The ballroom, the whole wing, in truth, was at once closed. Everything was left exactly as it was on that fatal night. A few years ago, the house being unexpectedly full, I opened the room in which you have been staying, and it has been used from time to time as a guest-room since. My son lived some years, prematurely old, heart-broken, and desolate. He died with her name on his lips."

Madame Arnault stopped.

A suffocating sensation was creeping over her listener. Only in the past few moments had the signification of the story begun to dawn upon him. "Do you mean," he gasped, "that the girl whom I —that she is—was—"

"Hélène, the dead wife of Félix Arnault," she replied, gravely. "Her restless spirit has walked here before. I have sometimes heard her tantalizing laugh echo through the house, but no one had ever seen her until you came—so like the Richard Keith she loved!"

"When I read your letter," she went on, after a short silence, "which told me that you wished to come to those friends to whom your father had been so dear, all the past arose before me, and I felt that I ought to forbid your coming. But I remembered how Félix and Richard had loved each other before she came between

them. I thought of the other Richard
Keith whom I—I loved once; and I
dreamed of a union at last between the
families. I hoped, Richard, that you and
Félice—"

But Richard was no longer listening.
He wished to believe the whole fantastic
story an invention of the keen-eyed old
madame herself. Yet something within
him confessed to its truth. A tumultuous
storm of baffled desire, of impotent anger,
swept over him. The ring he wore burned into his flesh. But he had no thought
of removing it—the ring which had once
belonged to the beautiful golden-haired
woman who had come back from the
grave to woo him to her!

He turned his face away and groaned.

Her eyes hardened. She rose stiffly.
"I will send a servant with your breakfast," she said, with her hand on the door.
"The down boat will pass La Glorieuse
this afternoon. You will perhaps wish to
take advantage of it."

He started. He had not thought of going—of leaving her—*her!* He looked at
the portrait on the wall and laughed bitterly.

Madame Arnault accompanied him with
ceremonious politeness to the front steps
that afternoon.

"Mademoiselle Félice?" he murmured, inquiringly, glancing back at the windows of the sitting-room.

"Mademoiselle Arnault is occupied," she coldly returned. "I will convey to her your farewell."

He looked back as the boat chugged away. Peaceful shadows enwrapped the house and overspread the lawn. A single window in the wing gleamed like a bale-fire in the rays of the setting sun.

The years that followed were years of restless wandering for Richard Keith. He visited his estate but rarely. He went abroad and returned, hardly having set foot to land; he buried himself in the fastnesses of the Rockies; he made a long, aimless sea-voyage. Her image accompanied him everywhere. Between him and all he saw hovered her faultless face; her red mouth smiled at him; her white arms enticed him. His own face became worn and his step listless. He grew silent and gloomy. "He is madder than the old colonel, his father, was," his friends said, shrugging their shoulders.

One day, more than three years after his visit to La Glorieuse, he found himself on a deserted part of the Florida sea-coast. It was late in November, but the sky was soft and the air warm and balmy.

He bared his head as he paced moodily to
and fro on the silent beach. The waves
rolled languidly to his feet and receded,
leaving scattered half-wreaths of opales-
cent foam on the snowy sands. The wind
that fanned his face was filled with the
spicy odors of the sea. Seized by a capri-
cious impulse, he threw off his clothes and
dashed into the surf. The undulating
billows closed around him; a singular
lassitude passed into his limbs as he
swam; he felt himself slowly sinking, as
if drawn downward by an invisible hand.
He opened his eyes. The waves lapped
musically above his head; a tawny glory
was all about him, a luminous expanse in
which he saw strangely formed creatures
moving, darting, rising, falling, coiling,
uncoiling.

"You was jes on de eedge er drownd-
in', Mars Dick," said Wiley, his black
body-servant, spreading his own clothes
on the porch of the little fishing-hut to
dry. "In de name o' Gawd whar mek you
wanter go in swimmin' dis time o' de
yea', anyhow? Ef I hadn' er splunge in
an' fotch you out, dey'd er been mo'nin'
yander at de plantation, sho!"

His master laughed lazily. "You are
right, Wiley," he said; "and you are going to smoke the best tobacco in Maryland

as long as you live." He felt buoyant.
Youth and elasticity seemed to have come
back to him at a bound. He stretched
himself on the rough bench, and watched
the blue rings of smoke curl lightly away
from his cigar. Gradually he was aware
of a pair of wistful eyes shining down on
him. His heart leaped. They were the
eyes of Félice Arnault! "My God, have
I been mad!" he muttered. His eyes
sought his hand. The ring, from which
he had never been parted, was gone. It
had been torn from his finger in his wres-
tle with the sea. "Get my traps together
at once, Wiley," he said. "We are going
to La Glorieuse."

"Now you *talkin'*, Mars Dick," assent-
ed Wiley, cheerfully.

It was night when he reached the city.
First of all, he made inquiries concerning
the little packet. He was right; the *As-
sumption* would leave the next afternoon
at five o'clock for Bayou L'Eperon. He
went to the same hotel at which he had
stopped before when on his way to La
Glorieuse. The next morning, too joyous
to sleep, he rose early, and went out into
the street. A gray uncertain dawn was
just struggling into the sky. A few people on their way to market or to early
mass were passing along the narrow ban-

quettes; sleepy-eyed women were unbar-
ring the shutters of their tiny shops; high-
wheeled milk-carts were rattling over the
granite pavements; in the vine-hung
court-yards, visible here and there through
iron *grilles,* parrots were scolding on their
perches; children pattered up and down
the long, arched corridors; the prolonged
cry of an early clothes-pole man echoed,
like the note of a winding horn, through
the close alleys. Keith sauntered carelessly along.

"In so many hours," he kept repeating
to himself, "I shall be on my way to La
Glorieuse. The boat will swing into the
home landing; the negroes will swarm
across the gang-plank, laughing and
shouting; Madame Arnault and Félice will
come out on the gallery and look, shading
their eyes with their hands. Oh, I know
quite well that the old madame will greet
me coldly at first. Her eyes are like steel
when she is angry. But when she knows
that I am once more a sane man—
And Félice, what if she— But no!
Félice is not the kind of woman who loves
more than once; and she did love me,
God bless her! unworthy as I was."

A carriage, driven rapidly, passed him;
his eyes followed it idly, until it turned
far away into a side street. He strayed on

to the market, where he seated himself
on a high stool in *L'Appel du Matin* coffee stall. But a vague, teasing remembrance was beginning to stir in his brain.
The turbaned woman on the front seat of
the carriage that had rolled past him yonder, where had he seen that dark, grave,
wrinkled face, with the great hoops of
gold against either cheek? *Marcelite!*
He left the stall and retraced his steps,
quickening his pace almost to a run as he
went. Félice herself, then, might be in
the city. He hurried to the street into
which the carriage had turned, and
glanced down between the rows of white-
eaved cottages with green doors and batten shutters. It had stopped several
squares away; there seemed to be a number of people gathered about it. "I will
at least satisfy myself," he thought.

As he came up, a bell in a little cross-
crowned tower began to ring slowly. The
carriage stood in front of a low red brick
house, set directly on the street; a silent
crowd pressed about the entrance. There
was a hush within. He pushed his way
along the banquette to the steps. A
young nun, in a brown serge robe, kept
guard at the door. She wore a wreath of
white artificial roses above her long coarse
veil. Something in his face appealed to

her, and she found a place for him in the
little convent chapel.

Madame Arnault, supported by Marcelite, was kneeling in front of the altar,
which blazed with candles. She had
grown frightfully old and frail. Her face
was set, and her eyes were fixed with a
rigid stare on the priest who was saying mass. Marcelite's dark cheeks were
streaming with tears. The chapel, which
wore a gala air with its lights and flowers, was filled with people. On the left of
the altar, a bishop, in gorgeous robes, was
sitting, attended by priests and acolytes;
on the right, the wooden panel behind an
iron grating had been removed, and beyond, in the nun's choir, the black-robed
sisters of the order were gathered. Heavy
veils shrouded their faces and fell to their
feet. They held in their hands tall wax-
candles, whose yellow flames burned
steadily in the semi-darkness. Five or
six young girls knelt, motionless as stat-
ues, in their midst. They also carried ta-
pers, and their rapt faces were turned
towards the unseen altar within, of which
the outer one is but the visible token.
Their eyelids were downcast. Their white
veils were thrown back from their calm
foreheads, and floated like wings from
their shoulders.

He felt no surprise when he saw Félice among them. He seemed to have fore-known always that he should find her thus on the edge of another and mysteri-ous world into which he could not follow her.

Her skin had lost a little of its warm rich tint; the soft rings of hair were drawn away under her veil; her hands were thin, and as waxen as the taper she held. An unearthly beauty glorified her pale face.

" Is it forever too late ?" he asked him-self in agony, covering his face with his hands. When he looked again the white veil on her head had been replaced by the sombre one of the order. " If I could but speak to her !" he thought; " if she would but once lift her eyes to mine, she would come to me even now !"

Félice! Did the name break from his lips in a hoarse cry that echoed through the hushed chapel, and silenced the voice of the priest? He never knew. But a faint color swept into her cheeks. Her eyelids trembled. In a flash the rose-garden at La Glorieuse was before him; he saw the turquoise sky, and heard the mellow chorus of the field gang; the smell of damask-roses was in the air; her little hand was in his . . . he saw her

coming swiftly towards him across the
dusk of the old ballroom; her limpid innocent eyes were smiling into his own
... she was standing on the grassy lawn;
the shadows of the leaves flickered over
her white gown. . . .

At last the quivering eyelids were lifted. She turned her head slowly, and
looked steadily at him. He held his
breath. A cart rumbled along the cob-
ble-stones outside; the puny wail of a
child sounded across the stillness; a handful of rose leaves from a vase at the foot
of the altar dropped on the hem of Madame Arnault's dress. It might have
been the gaze of an angel in a world
where there is no marrying nor giving in
marriage, so pure was it, so passionless,
so free of anything like earthly desire.

As she turned her face again towards
the altar the bell in the tower above
ceased tolling; a triumphant chorus leaped into the air, borne aloft by joyous or-
gan tones. The first rays of the morning sun streamed in through the small
windows. Then light penetrated into the
nuns' choir, and enveloped like a mantle
of gold Sister Mary of the Cross, who in
the world had been Félicité Arnault.

A Faded Scapular

BY F. D. MILLET

W E are seldom able to trace our individual superstitions to any definite cause, nor can we often account for the peculiar sensations developed in us by the inexplicable and mysterious incidents in our experience. Much of the timidity of childhood may be traced to early training in the nursery, and sometimes the moral effects of this weakness cannot be eradicated through a lifetime of severe self-control and mental suffering. The complicated disorders of the imagination which arise from superstitious fears can frequently be accounted for only by inherited characteristics, by peculiar sensitiveness to impressions, and by an overpowering and perhaps abnormally active imagination. I am sure I am confessing to no unusual characteristic when I say that I have felt from childhood a certain sentiment or sensation in regard to material things which I

can trace to no early experience, to the
influence of no literature, and to no possible source, in fact, but that of inherited
disposition.

The sentiment I refer to is this: whatever has belonged to or has been used by
any person seems to me to have received
some special quality, which, though often
invisible and still oftener indefinable,
still exists in a more or less strong degree according to the amount of the im-
pressionable power, if I may call it so,
which distinguished the possessor. I am
aware that this sentiment may be stig-
matized as of the school-girl order; that
it is, indeed, of the same kind and class
with that which leads an otherwise honest person to steal a rag from a famous
battle flag, a leaf from a historical laurel
wreath, or even to cut a signature or a
title-page from a precious volume; but
with me the feeling has never taken this
turn, else I should never have confessed
to the possession of it. Whatever may
be said or believed, however, I must refer
to it in more or less comprehensible
terms, because it may explain the condi-
tions, although it will not unveil the
causes, of the incidents I am about to describe with all honesty and frankness.

Nearly twenty years ago I made my

first visit to Rome, long before it became
the centre of the commercial and politi-
cal activity of Italy, and while it was yet
unspoiled for the antiquarian, the stu-
dent, the artist, and the traveller. Never
shall I forget the first few hours I spent
wandering aimlessly through the streets,
so far as I then knew a total stranger in
the city, with no distinct plan of remaining there, and with only the slight and
imperfect knowledge of the place that
one gains from the ordinary travellers'
descriptions. The streets, the houses, the
people, the strange sounds and stranger
sights, the life so entirely different from
what I had hitherto seen, all this interested me greatly. Far more powerful
and far more vivid and lasting, however,
was the impression of an inconceivable
number of presences—I hesitate to call
them spirits—not visible, of course, nor
tangible, but still oppressing me mentally and morally, exactly the same as my
physical self is often crushed and overpowered in a great assembly of people.
I walked about, visited the cafés and concert halls, and tried in various ways to
shake off the uncomfortable feeling of
ghostly company, but was unsuccessful,
and went to my lodgings much depressed
and nervous. I took my note-book, and

15 S. H. D.

wrote in it: "Rome has been too much
lived in.   Among the multitude of the
dead there is no room for the living."
It seemed then a foolish memorandum
to write, and now, as I look at the
half-effaced pencil lines, I wonder why I
was not ashamed to write it.   Yet there
it is before me, a witness to my sensations at the time, and the scrawl has even
now the power to bring up to me an unpleasantly vivid memory of that first
evening in Rome.

After a few days passed in visiting the
galleries and the regular sights of the
town, I began to look for a studio and
an apartment, and finally found one in
the upper story of a house on the Via di
Ripetta.   Before moving into the studio,
I met an old friend and fellow-artist, and
as there was room enough for two, gladly took him in with me.

The studio, with apartment, in the Via
di Ripetta was by no means unattrac-
tive.   It was large, well lighted, comfortably and abundantly furnished.   It
was, as I have said, at the top of the
house, the studio overlooked the Tiber,
and the sitting-room and double-bedded
sleeping - room fronted the street.   The
large studio window was placed rather
high up, so that the entrance door—a

wide, heavy affair, with large hinges and
immense complicated lock and a "judas"
—opened from the obscurity of the hall
directly under the large window into the
full light of the studio. The roof of the
house slanted from back to front, so that
the two rooms were lower studded than
the studio, and an empty space or low
attic opening into the studio above them
was partly concealed by an ample and
ragged curtain. The fireplace was in the
middle of the left wall as you entered
the studio; the door into the sitting-room
was in the further right-hand corner, and
the bedroom was entered by a door on
the right-hand wall of the sitting-room,
so that the bedroom formed a wing of
the studio and sitting-room, and from the
former, looking through two doors, the
bedroom window and part of the street
wall could be seen. Both the beds were
hidden from sight of any one in the studio, even when the doors were open.

The apartment was furnished in a way
which denoted a certain amount of liberality, but everything was faded and
worn, though not actually shabby or dirty.
The carpets were threadbare, the damask-
covered sofa and chairs showed marks of
the springs, and the gimp was fringed
and torn off in places. The beds were not

mates; the basin and ewer were of different patterns; the few pictures on the wall were, like everything else in the place, curiously gray and dusty-looking, as if they had been shut up in the darkened rooms for a generation. Beyond the fireplace in the studio, the corner of the room was partitioned off by a dingy screen, six feet high or more, fixed to the floor for the space of two yards, with one wing which shut like a door, enclosing a small space fitted up like a miniature scullery, with a curious and elaborate collection of pots and pans and kitchen utensils, all hung in orderly rows, but every article with marks of service on it, and more recent and obtrusive trace of long disuse.

In one of the first days of my search for a studio I had found and inspected this very place, but it had given me such a disagreeable feeling—it had seemed so worn out, so full of relics of other people —that I could not make up my mind to take it. After a thorough search and diligent inquiry, however, I came to the conclusion that there was absolutely no other place in Rome at that busy season where I could set up my easel, and after having the place recommended to me by all the artists I called upon as a well-

known and useful studio, and a great
find at the busy season of the year, I took
a lease of the place for four months.

My friend and I moved in at the same
time, and I will not deny that I planned
to be supported by the presence of my
friend at the moment of taking possession. When we arrived and had our
traps all deposited in the middle of the
studio, there came over the spirits of us
both a strange gloom, which the bustle
and confusion of settling did not in the
least dispel. It was nearly dark that
winter afternoon before we had finished
unpacking, and the street lights were
burning before we reached the little res-
taurant in the Via Quattro Fontano,
where we proposed to take our meals.
There was a cheerful company of artists
and architects assembled there that evening, and we sat over our wine long after
dinner. When the jolly party at last dis-
persed, it was well past midnight.

How gloomy the outer portal of the
high building looked as we crossed the
dimly lighted street and pushed open the
black door! A musty, damp smell, like
the atmosphere of the catacombs, met us
as we entered. Our footsteps echoed
loud and hollow in the empty corridor,
and the large wax match I struck as we

came in gave but a flickering light, which
dimly shadowed the outline of the stone
stairway, and threw the rest of the corridor into a deep and mysterious gloom.
We tramped up the five long flights of
stone stairs without a word, the echo of
our footsteps sounding louder and louder, and the murky space behind us deep-
ening into the damp darkness of a cavern.
At last, after what seemed an interminable climb, we came to the studio entrance.
I put the large key in the lock, turned it,
and pushed open the door. A strong
draught, like the lifeless breath from the
mouth of a tunnel, extinguished the
match and left us in darkness. I hesitated an instant, instinctively dreading
to enter, and then went in, followed by
my friend, who closed the door behind
us. The heavy hinges creaked, the door
shut into the jambs with a solid thud,
the lock sprang into place with a sharp
click, and a noise like the clanging of
a prison gate resounded and re-echoed
through the corridor and through the
spacious studio. I felt as if we were
shut in from the whole world.

Lighting all the candles at hand and
stirring up the fire, we endeavored to
make the studio look cheerful, and neither
of us being inclined to go to bed, we sat

for a long time talking and smoking.
But even the bright fire and the soothing
tobacco smoke did not wholly dispel the
gloom of the place, and when we finally
carried the candles into the bedroom, I
felt a vague sense of dismal anticipation
and apprehension. We left both doors
open, so that the light from our room
streamed across the corner of the sitting-
room, and threw a great square of strong
reflection on the studio carpet. While
undressing, I found that I had left my
match-box on the studio table, and
thought I would return for it. I remember now what a mental struggle I went
through before I made up my mind to go
without a candle. I glanced at my
friend's face, partly to see if he noticed
any indication of nervousness in my expression, and partly because I was conscious of a kind of psychological sympathy between us. But fear that he
would laugh at me made me effectually
conceal my feelings, and I went out of
the room without speaking. As I walked
across the non-resonant, carpeted stone
floor I had the most curious set of sensations I have ever experienced. At nearly every step I took I came into a different stratum or perpendicular layer of
air. First it was cool to my face, then

warm, then chill again, and again warm.
Thinking to calm my nervous excitement,
I stood still and looked around me. The
great window above my head dimly trans-
mitted the sky reflection, but threw little
light into the studio. The folds of the
curtain over the open space above the
sitting-room appeared to wave slightly in
the uncertain light, and the easels and
lay-figure stood gaunt and ghostly along
the further wall. I waited there and
reasoned with myself, arguing that there
was no possible cause for fear, that a
strong man ought to control his nerves,
that it was silly at my time of life to begin to be afraid of the dark, but I could
not get rid of the sensation. As I went
back to the bedroom I experienced the
same succession of physical shocks; but
whether they followed each other in the
same order or not I was unable to de-
termine.

It was some time before I could get to
sleep, and I opened my eyes once or
twice before I lost consciousness. From
the bedroom window there was a dim,
very dim light on the lace curtains, but
the window itself was visible as a square
mass, and did not appear to illuminate
the room in the least. Suddenly, after a
dreamless sleep of some duration, I awoke

as completely as if I had been startled by
a loud noise. The lace curtains were
now quite brilliantly lighted from somewhere, I could not tell where, but the
window itself seemed to be as little luminous as when I went to sleep. Without
moving my head, I turned my eyes in
the direction of the studio, and could see
the open door as a dark patch in the
gray wall, but nothing more. Then, as I
was looking again at the curious illumi-
nation of the curtains, a moving mass
came into the angle of my vision out of
the corner of the room near the head of
the bed, and passed slowly into full view
between me and the curtain. It was un-
mistakably the figure of a man, not unlike that of the better type of Italian,
and was dressed in the commonly worn
soft hat and ample cloak. His profile
came out clearly against the light background of the lace curtain, and showed
him to be a man of considerable refine-
ment of feature. He did not make an
actually solid black silhouette against the
light, neither was the figure translucent,
but was rather like an object seen through
a vapor or through a sheet of thin ground
glass.

I tried to raise my head, but my nerve
force seemed suddenly to fail me, and

while I was wondering at my powerless·
ness, and reasoning at the same time that
it must be a nightmare, the figure had
moved slowly across in front of the window, and out through the open door into
the studio.

I listened breathlessly, but not a sound
did I hear from the next room. I pinched
myself, opened and shut my eyes, and
noticed that the breathing of my roommate was irregular, and unlike that of a
sleeping man. I am unable to understand why I did not sit up or turn over
or speak to my friend to find out if he
was awake. I was fully conscious that
I ought to do this, but something, I
know not what, forced me to lie perfectly
motionless watching the window. I heard
my roommate breathing, opened and shut
my eyes, and was certain, indeed, that I
was really awake. As I reasoned on the
phenomenon, and came naturally to the
unwilling conclusion that my hallucination was probably premonitory of malaria,
my nerves grew quiet, I began to think
less intensely, and then I fell asleep.

The next morning I awoke with a feeling of disagreeable anticipation. I was
loath to rise, even though the warm
Italian sunlight was pouring into the
room and gilding the dingy interior

with brilliant reflections. In spite of this
cheering glow of sunshine, the rooms
still had the same dead and uninhabited
appearance, and the presence of my
friend, a vigorous and practical man,
seemed to bring no recognizable vitality
or human element to counteract the op-
pressiveness of the place. Every detail of
my waking dream or hallucination of the
night before was perfectly fresh in my
mind, and the sense of apprehension was
still strong upon me.

The distracting operations of settling
the studio, and the frequent excursions
to neighboring shops to buy articles necessary to our meagre housekeeping, did
much towards taking my mind off the incident of the night, but every time I
entered the sitting-room or the bedroom
it all came up to me with a vividness
that made my nerves quiver. We ex-
plored all the corners and cupboards of
the place. We even crawled up over the
sitting-room behind the dingy curtain,
where a large quantity of disused frames
and old stretchers were packed away.
We familiarized ourselves, in fact, with
every nook and cranny of each room;
moved the furniture about in a different
order; hung up draperies and sketches,
and in many ways changed the character

of the interior. The faded, weary-look-
ing widow from whom I hired the place,
and who took care of the rooms, carried
away to her own apartment many of the
most obnoxious trifles which encumbered
the small tables, the étagère, and the
wall spaces. She sighed a great deal as
we were making the rapid changes to
suit our own taste, but made no objection, and we naturally thought it was
the regular custom of every new occupant to turn the place upside down.

Late in the afternoon I was alone in
the studio for an hour or more, and sat
by the fire trying to read. The daylight
was not gone, and the rumble of the busy
street came plainly to my ears. I say
"trying to read," for I found reading
quite impossible. The moment I began
to fix my attention on the page, I had a
very powerful feeling that some one was
looking over my shoulder. Do what I
would, I could not conquer the unreason-
able sensation. Finally, after starting
up and looking about me a dozen times,
I threw down the book and went out.
When I returned, after an hour in the
open air, I found my friend walking up
and down in the studio with open doors
and two guttering candles alight.

"It's a curious thing," he said, "I

can't read this book. I have been trying
to put my mind on it a whole half-hour,
and I can't do it. I always thought I
could get interested in Gaborieau in a
moment under any circumstances."

"I went out to walk because I couldn't
manage to read," I replied, and the conversation ended.

We went to the theatre that evening,
and afterwards to the Café Greco, where
we talked art in half a dozen languages
until midnight, and then came home.
Our entrance to the house and the studio
was much the same as on the previous
night, and we went to bed without a
word. My mind naturally reverted to
the experience of the night before, and I
lay there for a long time with my eyes
open, making a strong effort of the imagination to account for the vision by
the dim shapes of the furniture, the lace
curtains, and the suggestive and shadowy
perspective. But, although the interior
was weird enough, by reason of the dingy
hangings and the diffused light, I was
unable to trace the origin of the illusion
to any object within the range of my
vision, or to account for the strange illu-
mination which had startled me. I went
to sleep thinking of other things, and
with my nerves comparatively quiet.

Some time in the early morning, about three o'clock, as near as I could judge, I slowly awoke, and saw the lace curtains illuminated as before. I found myself in an expectant frame of mind, neither calm nor excited, but rather in that condition of philosophical quiet which best prepared me for an investigation of the phenomenon which I confidently expected to witness. Perhaps this is assuming too eagerly the position of a philosopher, but I am certain no element of fear disturbed my reason, that I was neither startled nor surprised at awakening as I did, and that my mind was active and undoubtedly prepared for the investigation of the mystery.

I was therefore not at all shocked to observe the same shape come first into the angle of my eye, and then into the full range of my vision, next appear as a silhouette against the curtains, and finally lose itself in the darkness of the doorway. During the progress of the shape across the room I noticed the size and general aspect of it with keen attention to detail and with satisfactory calmness of observation. It was only after the figure had passed out of sight, and the light on the window curtains grew dim again, much as an electric light loses its brilliancy with the diminution of the strength of the current, that it occurred to me to consider the fact that during the period of the hallucination I had been utterly motionless. There was not the slightest doubt of my being awake. My friend in the adjoining bed was breathing regularly, the ticking of my watch was plainly audible, and I could feel my heart beating with unusual rapidity and vigor.

The strange part of the whole incident was this incapacity of action, and the more I reasoned about it the more I was mystified by the utter failure of nerve force. Indeed, while the mind was actively at work on this problem the physical torpor continued, a lanquor not unlike the incipient drowsiness of anæsthesia came gradually over me, and, though mentally protesting against the helpless condition of the body, and struggling to keep awake, I fell asleep, and did not stir till morning.

With the bright clear winter's day returned the doubts and disappointments of the day before—doubts of the existence of the phenomenon, disappointment at the failure of any solution of the hallucination. A second day in the studio did little towards dispelling the mental gloom which possessed us both, and at night my friend confessed that he thought we must have stumbled into a malarial quarter.

At this distance of time it is absolutely incomprehensible to me how I could have gone on as I did from day to day, or rather from night to night—for the same hallucination was repeated nightly —without speaking to my friend, or at least taking some energetic steps towards an investigation of the mystery. But I had the same experience every night for fully a week before I really began to plan serious means of discovering whether it was a hallucination, a nightmare, or a flesh - and - blood intruder. First, I had some curiosity each night to see whether there would be a repetition of the incident. Second, I was eager to note any physical or mental symptom which would serve as a clew to the mystery. Pride, or some other equally authoritative sentiment, continued to keep me from disclosing my secret to my friend, although I was on the point of doing so on several occasions. My first plan was to keep a candle burning all night, but I could invent no plausible excuse to my comrade for this action. Next I proposed to shut the bedroom door, and on speaking of it to my friend, he strongly objected on the ground of the lack of ventilation, and was not willing to risk having the window open on account of the malaria. After all, since this was an entirely personal matter, it seemed to me the only thing to do was to depend on my own strength of mind and moral courage to solve this mystery unaided. I put my loaded revolver on the table by the bedside, drew back the lace curtain before going to bed, and left the door only half open, so I could not see into the studio. The night I made these preparations I awoke as usual, saw the same figure, but, as before, could not move a hand. After it had passed the window, I tried hard to bring myself to take my revolver, and find out whether I had to deal with a man or a simulacrum. But even while I was arguing with myself, and trying to find out why I could not move, sleep came upon me before I had carried out my purposed action.

The shock of the first appearance of the vision had been nearly overbalanced by my eagerness to investigate, and my intense interest in the novel condition of mind or body which made such an experience possible. But after the utter failure of all my schemes and the col-

lapse of my theories as to evident causes
of the phenomenon, I began to be har-
assed and worried, almost unconsciously
at first, by the ever-present thought, the
daily anticipation, and the increasing
dread of the hallucination. The self-
confidence that first supported me in my
nightly encounter diminished on each
occasion, and the curiosity which stimu-
lated me to the study of the phenomenon
rapidly gave way to the sentiment akin
to terror when I proved myself incapable
of grappling with the mystery.

The natural result of this preoccupa-
tion was inability to work and little interest in recreation, and as the long
weeks wore away I grew morose, morbid, and hypochondriacal. The pride
which kept me from sharing my secret
with my friend also held me at my post
and nerved me to endure the torment in
the rapidly diminishing hope of finally
exorcising the spectre or recovering my
usual healthy tone of mind. The difficulty of my position was increased by
the fact that the apparition failed to appear occasionally, and while I welcomed
each failure as a sign that the visits were
to cease, they continued spasmodically
for weeks, and I was still as far away
from the interpretation of the problem

as ever. Once I sought medical advice,
but the doctor could discover nothing
wrong with me except what might be
caused by tobacco, and, following his advice, I left off smoking. He said I had
no malaria; that I needed more exercise,
perhaps; but he could not account for
my insomnia, for I, like most patients,
had concealed the vital facts in my case,
and had complained of insomnia as the
cause of my anxiety about my health.

The approach of spring tempted me
out-of-doors, and in the warm villa gardens and the sun-bathed Campagna I
could sometimes forget the nightmare
that haunted me. This was not often
possible unless I was in the company of
cheerful companions, and I grew to dread
the hour when I was to return to the
studio after an excursion into the country
among the soothing signs of returning
summer. To shut the clanging door of
the studio was to place an impenetrable
barrier between me and the outside
world, and the loneliness of that interior
seemed to be only intensified by the presence of my companion, who was apparently as much depressed in spirits as myself.

We made various attempts at the en-
tertainment of friends, but they all lacked that element of spontaneous fun

which makes such occasions successful, and we gave it up. On pleasant days we threw open the windows on the street to let in the warm air and sunshine, but this did not seem to drive away the musty odors of the interior. We were much too high up to feel any neighborly proximity to the people on the other side of the street. The chimney-pots and irregular roofs below and beyond were not very cheerful objects in the view, and the landlady, who, as far as we knew, was the only other occupant of the upper story, did not give us a great sense of companionship. Never once did I enter the studio without feeling the same curious sensation of alternate warm and cool strata of air. Never for a quarter of an hour did I succeed in reading a book or a newspaper, however interesting it might be. We frequently had two models at a time, and both my friend and myself made several beginnings of pictures, but neither of us carried the work very far.

On one occasion a significant remark was made by a lady friend who came to call. She will undoubtedly remember now when she reads these lines that she said, on leaving the studio: "This is a curiously draughty place. I feel as if it

had been blowing hot and cold on me
all the time I have been here, and yet
you have no windows open."

At another time my comrade burst out
as I was going away one evening about
eleven o'clock to a reception at one of
the palaces: "I wish you wouldn't go
in for society so much. I can't go to
the café; all the fellows go home about
this time of the evening. I don't like to
stay here in this dismal hole all cooped
up by myself. I can't read, I can't sleep,
and I can't think."

It occurred to me that it was a little
queer for him to object to being left
alone, unless he, like myself, had some
disagreeable experiences there, and I remembered that he had usually gone out
when I had, and was seldom, if ever,
alone in the studio when I returned. His
tone was so peevish and impatient that I
thought discussion was injudicious, and
simply replied, "Oh, you're bilious; I'll
be home early," and went away. I have
often thought since that it was the one
occasion when I could have easily broached the subject of my mental trouble, and
I have always regretted I did not do
so.

Matters were brought to a climax in
this way: My friend was summoned to

America by telegraph a little more than
two months after we took the studio, and
left me at a day's notice. The amount
and kind of moral courage I had to sum-
mon up before I could go home alone
the first evening after my comrade left
me can only be appreciated by those who
have undergone some similar torture.
It was not like the bracing up a man
goes through when he has to face some
imminent known danger, but was of a
more subtle and complex kind. "There
is nothing to fear," I kept saying to myself, and yet I could not shake off a
nameless dread. "You are in your right
mind and have all your senses," I continually argued, "for you see and hear
and reason clearly enough. It is a brief
hallucination, and you can conquer the
mental weakness which causes it by persistent strength of will. If it be a simulacrum, you as a practical man, with
good physical health and sound enough
reasoning powers, ought to investigate
it to the best of your ability." In this
way I endeavored to nerve myself up,
and went home late, as usual. The regular incident of the night occurred. I
felt keenly the loss of my friend's companionship, and suffered accordingly,
but in the morning I was no nearer to

the solution of the mystery than I was before.

For five weary, torturing nights did I go up to that room alone, and, with no sound of human proximity to cheer me or to break the wretched feeling of utter solitude, I endured the same experience. At last I could bear it no longer, and determined to have a change of air and surroundings. I hastily packed a travelling-bag and my color-box, leaving all my extra clothes in the wardrobes and the bureau drawers, told the landlady I should return in a week or two, and paid her for the remainder of the time in advance. The last thing I did was to take my travelling-cap, which hung near the head of my bed. A break in the wallpaper showed that there was a small door here. Pulling the knob which had held my cap, the door was readily opened, and disclosed a small niche in the wall. Leaning against the back of the niche was a small crucifix with a rude figure of Christ, and suspended from the neck of the image by a small cord was a triangular object covered with faded cloth. While I was examining with some interest the hiding-place of these relics, the landlady entered.

"What are these?" I asked.

" Oh, signore!" she said, half sobbing
as she spoke. " Those are relics of my
poor husband. He was an artist like
yourself, signore. He was—he was—ill,
very ill—and in mind as well as body,
signore. May the Blessed Virgin rest
his soul! He hated the crucifix, he hated
the scapular, he hated the priests. Signore, he—he died without the sacra-
ment, and cursed the holy water. I have
never dared to touch those relics, signore.
But he was a good man, and the best of
husbands"; and she buried her face in
her hands.

I took the first train for Naples, and
have never been in Rome since.

At the Hermitage

BY E. LEVI BROWN

THE October sun was shining hot, but it was cool and pleasant inside the mill. The brown water in Sawny Creek lapped softly against the rocks in its bed, and the sycamore and cottonwood trees, which grew from the water's edge up the steep, muddy banks, stood straight and motionless in the warm sunny air, no touch of autumn upon them yet; only the sweet - gums were turning slightly yellow, and the black-gums were tinging red. It wanted two hours of sunset, but blackbirds were on their way home, and the thickets were noisy with their crying.

Inside the moss-grown old mill there was music and dancing going on, for, comfortably reclining on a pile of cotton seed in the rough ginning - room, with thick festoons of cobwebs everywhere, and bits of dusty lint clinging to every splinter in its walls, a young man was playing a banjo, and two others, with

naked feet, were dancing as if for their
lives. A slim dark girl in a blue and
white homespun dress, her head turbaned
with a square of the same, sat on a bag of
seed cotton watching them.

"Now, boys, a break-down," called out
the player, "and then I must gin out Religion's cotton; come, now, lively."

And they went lively enough.

"You bake the bread, and gimme the crus';
You sift the meal, and gimme the husk;
You bile the pot, and gimme the grease;
I have the crumbs, and you have the feast—
But mis' gwine gimme the ham-bone."

The loose boards shook and trembled
under the heavy feet, the scattered cotton
seed whirled away in little eddies, and
baskets of cotton standing about tipped a
little break-down of their own. Even the
girl on the bag, whose sober, earnest face
seemed out of keeping with the gayety,
beat time with her bare feet. But by
the time the miller threw his banjo aside,
its strings still quivering, she was standing up, and the look of interest had given
place to the old gravity. She had not a
pretty feature, not even the usual pretty
teeth. She was a homely black girl.

"See here, Religion," said the miller,
"this here's Saturday evenin', and I keeps

holiday like everybody else but you; can't
you git along without that little tum of
cotton? It ain't wuth ginnin'."

"I'm 'bliged to have it," she answered.
"I didn't give nary day's work for rent
this week; will pay the week's rent and
git sumpin beside. We doesn't draw no
ration."

"It's a mighty small heap o' ration
you'll git out'n that tum of cotton after
you pay fifty cents for your week's rent.
Don't you find it cheaper to work out the
week's rent than to pay it?"

"I git fifty cents a hundred for pick-
in'," she answered, simply, "and I kin
pick two hundred and fifty a day, and
scrap twenty-five more. We doesn't git
but fifty cents fur a whole day's work on
the plantation."

He looked at her admiringly, at the
thin supple body and long light arms
that could reach so far among the cotton
bolls. He untied the bags and proceeded
to fill the gin. A girl who could pick
two hundred and seventy-five pounds of
cotton a day was a person of some con-
sequence.

The gin stopped its whir, and the clerk
weighed the cotton. Religion watched
him sharply, and counted the checks he
handed her twice.

"If you pass 'em at the Hermitage," he said, "tell 'em to give you another five-cent check; I'm short to-night."

"I ain't goin' to the Hermitage store; I'm goin' to the ferry. They give me cash there for the checks."

"What do they take off?"

"They takes one cent out'n every five. But I'm 'bliged to have the hard money. We has to pay for a good many things we git for Min in hard money." She had taken up the empty bags, but still waited. "I wish you'd please, sir, see if you 'ain't got another check nowhere."

"You're a sight, Religion," he said, good-naturedly. "Here's a nickel."

With her bags on her arm she went out across the dry grass to where a little black mule, not much larger than a goat, was standing. Beck greeted her with a bray astonishing for one of her size, and a switch with her rope of a tail. Un-heeding the cheerful greeting, Religion gave all her attention to untying the halter, and soon they were going along the sandy road straight through the woods.

The rickety box-wagon and the chain traces rattled noisily. Religion cracked her whip—it was a stick with a plaited leather string on the end. Beck was in

a hurry to get home, and the wagon
bumped along over roots and stumps
until it was a wonder how Religion kept
herself on the board which served for
a seat. All the swamps and woods in
Sawny were in bad repute. There was
an old cemetery, rambling over many
acres, lost in ivy and briers and immense
trees, but abundant in ghost stories.
There was the swamp through which
Sherman's soldiers had cut a road, and
near by was the hill - side where many
sunken hollows marked their graves. A
"spirit" could be raised there at a
thought's notice. Beck flew past these
unpleasant places, and her little hoofs
were clattering over the loose bridge at
the foot of the hill, where, the cemetery
ending, the plantation road began, when
she backed suddenly — so suddenly that
the board tipped up and dropped Religion
into the bottom of the wagon.

Beck had some tricks like all of her
kind, and thinking this was one, Religion
was scrambling up and readjusting her
seat when she saw a face bending over
her that she never forgot—a strange evil
face, the lower part hidden by a short
bushy beard, the upper by many thin
braids of hair curling at the ends. Between the two crops of hair she saw a

pair of small red eyes, dull and sleepy,
but with a curious gleam in them like
the eyes of the snakes in the swamp,
and thick widespread nostrils. She only
had time to note these features and the
thick rings of gold in the great ears
when the face disappeared, and, as if
they floated in the air, she heard the
words:

"I am the seventh son of the seventh
daughter. I know all things. I can tell
you what is killing your sister."

Religion pulled up her rope reins, and
Beck flew up the road as if all Sherman's army were after her; nor did she
slacken until she reached the great gate-
way which turned into the Hermitage.
Only a flat-topped post remained of the
gate, and a boy of twelve, with a face like
Religion's, was perched on it.

"Hi, dar, 'Ligion! Ho, Beck!" he
cried. "Take me in an' give me a piece
of a ride anyway," and with a twinkle of
his long ashy legs he landed safely in the
wagon.

"What you doin' here, Bud?" questioned his sister. "Why ain't you to
home with mammy and Min?"

"Min done had one o' she wussest
spells, an' mammy sent me to Miss Tina
fur calomel. I heerd youna comin', an'

I waited; 'kase ridin' beats walkin' black
and blue."

He looked up at her with a sly giggle,
and crammed his mouth with persim-
mons. He expected a scolding for delaying with the calomel, but his sister only
said:

" Quit eatin' them 'simmons. Pres'n'y
we'll have to git calomel for youna."

They were passing through the quarter
now, where every one was getting supper.
The air was full of the appetizing odor of
frying corn-bread and bacon and boiling
coffee. Men sat on the door - steps or
smoked in groups under the fine oaks
which grew in the middle of the street,
waiting for the call to supper. Up at the
end of the row of houses, and separated a
little from them by a wild-plum thicket,
stood a house like a black stump just seen
above the green around it. It had what
none of the others possessed, a porch in
front, but the rotten frame - work had
dropped off piece by piece, until it was a
mystery how the heavy scuppernong vine
that grew upon it was supported. There
were lilies and roses in the clean bit of
front yard, and on a box was a number of
geraniums flourishing in tin cans. There
were boxes of violets, and a thick honeysuckle was hugging a post and sending

out sweet yellow sprays. Beck drew up
before the house with a jerk that had determination in it. Bud jumped out with
a boyish shout, but his sister caught his
arm.

"Hush, Bud! Don't you hear Min?"

"Min made up that piece to-day," responded Bud, in a roaring whisper.
"Maw an' me's been scared pretty nigh to
death. Miss Tina say it ain't Min singin', but that spell workin' on her."

The voice was sweet and rich, with an
undercurrent of sadness running through
that went to the heart. It seemed to wait
and tremble, then float and float away,
dying into softest melody. It was not the
untaught music of the plantation singers;
it was a voice exquisitely trained.

"Lord! Lord!" ejaculated Religion.
The words held a heartful of trouble.
She lowered the shafts gently and led
Beck round the house.

"That you, Religion?" inquired a voice
from somewhere in the yard.

She could hear milk straining into a
pail, and the tramp of some animal over
dry shucks.

"It's me, maw, an' I got enough to pay
the rent, and there'll be some over."

"Youna mus' had good luck. Min 'll
be more'n middlin' glad of a few crackers.

I thought sure the gal was gone to-day,
Religion," and a tall form rose up from
beside the cow and came towards the girl.
" I sut'n'y thought she was gone to-day,"
continued the mother. " She just died
off, and didn't 'pear to have no more life
in her than a dead bird. I was mighty
scared."

" Why youna didn't send fur me ?"

" Chile, I didn't want to worry youna.
Then the neighbors come in, 'kase I did a
big piece o' hollerin', an' they worked on
her and fotched her back; I 'ain't been no
'count since. See how my hand trembles
now."

She placed her hand on her daughter's
arm. It was large and hard, but all the
ploughing, hoeing, and wood-cutting that
she had done had not destroyed its fine
shape. It was cold and trembling.

Religion took it between her own square
thick ones. " Never mind, maw; she's
better now, 'kase she's singin' a new
piece. I'll go an' eat and do the errands,
so as to git back. You won't feel so bad
when I'm here."

The single thing which made the room
she entered different from all the other
rooms in the quarter was a white bed.
The two other beds had the usual patch-
work quilts and yellow slips. Religion

17 S. H. D.

touched a light-wood splinter to the fire,
and holding the light above her head,
went up to the white bed. The face
on the pillow was of that pure lustrous
whiteness which is sometimes seen in
very young children; the features were
perfect. She seemed a creature of an entirely different sphere—as different from
Religion as a butterfly from a grub, and
yet there was an indefinable likeness between the two.

"I was waiting for you, 'Ligion," she
said, opening her eyes; "I want to tell
you something; come close, so ma and
Bud won't hear. A woman has been
here, a little old woman, and she sat on
the bed and told me some things. She
told me that Tina had cut off a piece of
my hair and hid it in a gum-tree in the
swamp, and that I never would be well
till my hair was found.

"I remember the night she combed my
hair, and how Mauma Amy said it was
bad luck to comb hair after dark; it was
so thick and long then, and it has come
out so since." She drew the long thin
brown braid between her fingers. "Why
should Tina want to hurt me? The only
harm I ever did her was to love her."

She burst into tears, and Religion
hugged her in mute sympathy; that was

her only way to comfort. When Min
was quiet, she stirred up the pillows and
smoothed out the white spread. Then
she took a tin cup full of clabber, poured
a little syrup upon it, and ate it heartily.
A plate of greens was hot on the hearth,
and a corn-cake was browning beautifully
in the bake-kettle. But there was no time
to eat the dainties.

John Robinson, the owner of Hermitage, was a single man. He was old,
feeble, and notoriously grasping, yet the
dirty, ill-smelling room which Religion
entered was strewn with choicest books,
sheets of music lay on the table and
chairs, and several rare violins lay on a
piano, whose mother-of-pearl keys glowed
in the red firelight.

"Who's that?" he called, in a cracked
old voice, the instant he heard Religion's
footsteps. He was wrapped in a cloak
and sunk in an arm-chair before the fire.

"Me, Marse John—Minnie's Religion.
I've come to pay the rent."

"Oh, come in, girl! Down, Bull!" he
piped to a great hound that was slowly
rising from a sheepskin. "It's fifty cents.
Sure you've got it all, and no nickels with
holes in them?"

She placed a little tobacco-bag in his
hand, and he leaned forward to the light

to count the money. He had a sharp,
pinched old face surrounded by shaggy
white hair. A portrait of him taken in a
long-past day hung over the fireplace. In
that he was a handsome man, with thick
chestnut-brown hair. His hands shook
so that the pieces of money dropped from
them and rolled upon the brick hearth.
A tall mulatto woman came from a near
room and picked them up.

"Count it over again, Tina," he com-
manded, "and see if it's all there and no
holes in it. You can't trust Religion
herself with money. How's your sister?"

"Min ain't no better; she ain't never
going to be no better in this world."

"Tut, tut!" he muttered. "There
should be some strength of will in that
girl. But, pshaw! she had a mother and
a line of nonentities behind her. I forgot that. Is that money all right, Tina?"

"It's all right, Marse John."

Tina was a beautiful woman, with the
smoothest brown skin, and black hair
coiled many times around a perfectly
shaped head.

The renters never waited long in Mr.
Robinson's presence when their business
was ended. But Religion only moved
back a little and lingered. Tina, bringing a cup of cocoa, at last noticed her.

"Why, Religion, you're not gone."

"And why ain't you gone!" screamed
the old man.

"I—I'm waiting for the receipt, sir."

"Waiting for the receipt?" he shrieked.
"God and fury! things have come to a
pretty pass that a slave wench should
wait in my house for a receipt. Get out
of this, or— Bull!"

"Stand still, Religion," cried Tina, as
the dog leaped up. "Down, Bull! Marse
John"—and her voice sank to a sweet,
soothing tone—"you'd better not upset
yourself so; you'll be sick."

She stroked his face and hair tenderly,
and when he lay back quiet in his chair,
worn out with his passion, she beckoned
to Religion to follow her. They went
into one of the rooms. The candle burning in it showed a bed, with posts reaching to the ceiling, and an ancient mahog-
any chest. A handful of fire burned in
the deep fireplace, and before it crouched
Mack, an old slave of Mr. Robinson's—
a miserable idiot, with just mind enough
to perform a very few menial services.

"Trick yer! trick yer!" he piped, in a
high thin voice, like an old woman's.
"Done got de blacksnake's head an' de
dead baby's hand right hyar. Trick yer!
trick yer! Git out quick!" He kept up

the cry while Tina wrote the receipt, and when she led the way to the door he pattered after them. "Git out quick, 'fore Tina trick yer. I done hope Tina trick Min."

Religion turned fiercely. "Has you tricked my sister and brung her to what she is?"

Tina laughed contemptuously. "Who says I put a spell on Min?"

"Min says it, an' Mack says it, an' I b'lieves it. You always was jealous of her, 'kase Marse John taught her, and made more of her than he did of you."

"Then it's likely this *spell* will put her out of my way," said Tina, all the sweetness gone out of her voice and face, and nothing but venom left. She turned to go in, but Religion dropped on her knees and clasped her feet.

"Oh, Tina! if you did put a spell on Min, take it off, for Christ's sake. Nobody kin do it but you. Our pooty, pooty Min! she be dyin' there before our eyes, and we-uns can't do nothin'. Take the ban off, an' I'll work for you the longest day I live."

Tina dragged herself away and shut the door heavily.

Religion was in the field scattering

pine straw, and Beck was there too, har-
nessed in company with a very lean Texas
pony. Her mother and Bud were in the
same occupation, but Mollie, the old
brown cow, drew their wagon.

Religion was crooning a solemn old
ditty, as she always did when alone and
thinking.

" I just made up my mind this mornin'
that I'd got to do sumpin when Mr. Frye
come for we-uns to scatter this straw.
An' I wish I knowed what to do. Oh,
Lord, don't I wish I knowed what to do.
There's Min been down on that air bed
one whole year come Christmas, and nobody can't say what is the matter with
her. Sich a heap o' calomel, and quinine,
and turpentine, and doctor's stuff as she
has took, and 'tain't done no good. I
can't count the times I been to the tavern.
I know I brung off more'n two gallons of
the best whiskey, an' it's been mixed up
with pine-top, an' snakeroot, an' mullein,
an' I dun'no' what all, an' none of it 'ain't
done no good. An' Min is dyin' just as
fast as she can die. Oh, Lord!"

A fine mule, drawing a light road-cart,
trotted past. The driver was a short,
squat man, his face almost hidden in hair.
It was Dr. Buzzard. He was known for
miles as a successful " conjurer " and

giver of "hands." Most of the people
around had perfect faith in his cures and
revelations, and had advised Religion to
try him, but the girl objected, vaguely
questioning reason and conscience, and
Min was getting worse. It was despair,
not belief, which made her whisper to
herself, "I'm goin' to see him this very
night."

"Great day! 'ain't we-uns had trouble!
Lord, Lord! I b'lieve one-half this wurl'
has all the trouble fur all the rest, anyhow!"

Religion was on her way, and thinking over the family record as she walked.
The sun had set, the cotton-pickers were
in, and odors of supper were afloat. Religion was eating hers as she walked and
thought—it was a finely browned ash-
cake, richly flavored with the cabbage
leaves in which it was baked.

The Beckets had always been very poor,
hard-working people, without any especial grace or finer touch of nature about
them. The two brothers had married two
sisters, and such marriages were considered unlucky.

When Religion was a little girl her father broke his contract with his employer,
and to escape imprisonment he ran away.
Religion remembered his stolen visits at

night, and his silent caresses of her. After a while the visits stopped. They heard
of him in a distant city, but he never
came back. His brother had died long
before.

The widowed sisters stayed on the plantation, and both were favorites of Mr.
Robinson. Min and Tina were half-sis-
ters. They were as opposite in character
as they were in appearance; everybody
loved Min; she sang like a bird, and her
voice had been carefully trained, and
some especial provision had been made for
its further cultivation when this strange
sickness overtook her.

Good nursing was unknown on the
plantations, or perhaps the slight cold,
which was the beginning of the end with
Min, might have been cured. Since no
member of the family had died with con-
sumption, it was not believed that she
could have it.

When all the home remedies and doctors' prescriptions failed, there was but
one verdict, Min was "hurt." It was
known that her half-sister was not very
friendly nor over-scrupulous, and it was
believed that Tina, out of jealousy, had
thrown an evil spell.

The light was still lingering when Religion, turning out of the road, ran down

a narrow lane bordered with turpentine
woods on one side, and on the other by a
field of dead pines. Away back among
the latter was a substantial log house,
with good brick chimneys at either end.
There were several smaller buildings in
the yard, and in one a woman was stooping over the fire frying cakes, a young
man was thrumming a banjo, and a little
boy in scantiest jeans was careening
around to the inspiring strains of " Old
Joe kicking up behind and before."

Inside, the large low-ceiled room was
in a blaze of light. There was a tumbled
bed in one corner, a table covered with
dusty dishes and glass-ware in another,
and a large case filled with bottles, jugs,
and bundles occupied a third. Walls and
ceiling were hidden by packages of herbs
and strings of roots, while over the fireplace were three shelves piled high with
cigar-boxes, carefully labelled.

Half buried in a great chair, his breast
bare, his sleeves rolled up above his elbows, the veins in his arms standing out
like cords, his legs wrapped in a blanket
and resting upon a stool, sat Dr. Buzzard,
to all appearances in a deep sleep. On
the floor, close to the hearth, was a most
evil-looking old crone, continually stirring a pot bubbling on the coals. She

threw one glance at Religion, and went
on stirring. The doctor never moved.
A splendid - looking mulatto noiselessly
brought a box, and the girl subsided upon
it.

There were other visitors. A young
man wanted help to get money that was
due him; another sought assistance in
settling a difficulty. A woman with a
child in her arms wanted to charm her
recreant husband back to her; a sick one
desired relief from the spell which was
making her cough her life out.

But the great man slumbered on with
a gentle snore, and the old woman stirred
the pot. There was not a sound in the
room save his snore, the swish of the
spoon, and the occasional dropping of a
coal. Every one sat in silent, intense
expectation, waiting for—they knew not
what.

The oaken logs had died down to a bed
of glowing coals when suddenly a red
glare flashed from it. Religion closed
her eyes, blinded by the light. When
she opened them the doctor was sitting
upright, his head hanging back, his eyes
wide open and staring upward, and his
breast heaving as if in pain. His wife
was in the room holding whispered con-
sultations with each person. The men

stated their complaints briefly, but the women detained her longer. When she had been the round she glided back to the side of the doctor.

Then in a low chant, sweet and sorrowful, she repeated the story which each had told her, running them into a continuous recitative. The old woman rose from the floor, and joining in the chant in a quavering croon, sprinkled salt at the thresholds of the doors and at the feet of every person, ending by throwing a large handful up the chimney. It fell back and sputtered and cracked in the fire. Seizing one of the cigar-boxes, she sprinkled a pinch of its contents over the fire. A dense gray vapor rose. The doctor raised his arms, and let them fall slowly, three times.

"The fire holds many secrets," he uttered, in a hollow, unnatural voice, like one talking in his sleep; "he who would see his enemy about his work of destruction, let him look in the fire."

With eyes ready to start from her head, Religion with the rest bent forward to look. She saw, or thought she saw, in the curling gray cloud a woman's face. It seemed to take shape and expression, as she gazed, until it grew familiar. The forsaken woman, who had seen the face

of a successful rival, sank heavily upon
the floor. Some of the others screamed,
some moaned and prayed. The cloud
over the fire was repeated many times,
and dissolving into fantastic shapes, pict-
ured to the excited fancy of the others
their enemies and distresses. At last the
exhibition ended, and the visitors were
sent from the room, and called in again,
separately, to receive directions, medi-
cines, and charms against further evil.

Religion found the doctor sitting at the
table, surrounded by jugs, bottles, and
boxes, his wife and the old woman standing on either side. He still slept, breathing heavily. His hands were on the
table.

"A girl named Religion Becket inquir-
ing for her sister," spoke the doctor in
the same strange voice. "The sister
seems to be dying."

"Say yes close to his right ear," in-
structed the wife, and Religion did so.

"The doctors know nothing about the
case," responded the conjurer. "A red
scorpion is inside her body feeding on her
vitals. I see a woman hiding something
in a black-gum tree that hangs over running water. It is at the hour when spirits
walk. The first creature that runs over
the cleft where the hand is hidden is the

one to torment your sister. That first
creature is a red scorpion. Its young one
lives in your sister's side. I, even I, can
withdraw it."

Like one moved by some power outside
of himself, his hands moved in the array
before him, lightly touching this or that
bottle and bundle until he found what
he sought. And like a careful druggist
he deliberately measured each ingredient,
giving clear directions at the same time.
When Religion came out she had a large
bottle of medicine, several huge plasters,
and orders for a bewildering list of root
teas, with a promise of an early visit
from the great man himself.

Religion was feeding the cane - mill.
Bud was on the other side drawing out
the crushed cane; the mother was under
the shed stirring the boiling syrup. Beck
was travelling round and round doing
the grinding. The sun was set. It would
soon be time to stop work. Religion
seemed to be expecting some one; she
never stooped to pick up an armful of
stalks without glancing up the road.

"What you keep lookin' up the road
for, 'Ligion?" inquired her mother, her
body swaying back and forth as she drew
or pushed the long wooden ladle.

"Nuthin.' I ain't lookin' fur nuthin'."

"I b'lieve there's a spell on youna too," said her mother, surveying her anxiously. "I wish youna 'd be more keerful and not put your fingers so close to the teeth."

"It's time to quit, anyhow," put in Bud; "the sun's 'way down, an' I'm more'n middlin' hungry."

"You kin take the mule out an' go home an' make the fire. Will you go an' git supper, Religion, or stay an' stir?"

"I reckon I'll stay and stir. You kin bring me some supper when you come. We'll be here half the night."

With another look up the road, where the sunlight was fast fading, she took up the wet bags which protected her dress, and passed under the shed, glad to sit down and rest her aching limbs. The shed was a primitive affair, but everything was convenient for syrup-boiling, and the two long boilers were full of the golden-brown liquid. There was nothing to do but to stir continually and keep a steady fire.

The short autumn twilight had died out, and the fields and woods were slipping into gloom. The cane-mill was in the overseer's yard, and back of it the quarter began. A multitude of sounds

came up to Religion's ear—the crying of
babies, the laughing of children, the barking of dogs, the whistle of the boys rubbing off the mules, the scolding and calling of women for wood and water. Night
was closing in. Religon stirred and
thought.

All Dr. Buzzard's instructions had been
carefully followed. He had come many
times, performed a variety of strange operations, frightened and gladdened them
all one day by declaring that the red scorpion had passed out of her body through
her foot and run into the fire, that now
all danger was passed, pocketed thirty
dollars which Minnie and Religion had
obtained by giving a lien on Beck, the
old cow, all the corn in the crib, and every article of furniture their cabin held;
and still Min was no better—was worse,
indeed, with the worry of it all.

Some one was coming. "Is that you,
Bud?" she called.

The unnatural laugh that answered her
could belong to no one but Mack. Lift-
ing a blazing stick above her head, she
peered out into the darkness.

"Come fur youna," he mumbled.
"Miss Tina goin' on drefful; come fur
youna quick."

"You go, Religion," said a woman

who had come unperceived. " The Lord's
gwine to cl'ar up some t'ings what's took
place in this quarter. You go, an' I'll
stay an' stir."

Religion hurried away. She found
Tina tossing about in a pretty white bed,
her hands and feet bound in onions, her
whole body swathed in red flannel satu-
rated with turpentine, and her head band-
aged with dock leaves wet with vinegar.
There was a hot fire, and the room was
crowded with men and women.

Dr. Buzzard was there, with a black
calico bag, from which he frequently
drew a black bottle, examined it sharply
at the lamp, then gravely replaced it,
after which he always looked at and
pinched Tina's fingers.

" Mother," he said at last, addressing
himself to Tina's mother, " the time has
come for me to show you the cause of
your daughter's illness. She has been
hurt. She was too beautiful and well
loved to suit all I could name. An evil
hand was laid on her."

He took out his watch, looked at it
gravely, and laid it upon the table. Removing his coat, he turned back the cuffs
of his brown shirt, then took off the
bandages from Tina's hands and feet.

He rubbed each arm from the shoulder

18 S. H. D.

to the end of the fingers with one sweep, first lightly, then harder, snapping his fingers violently after every stroke. Tina writhed under the treatment, then screamed loudly, and tried to leap from the bed. He called two men to hold her, and the rubbing went on.

With each stroke he grew more and more excited. He lifted his arms high above his head, and bore down upon Tina painfully. His eyes were burning, and the perspiration pouring down his face. He broke into a low humming, and the women took it up, moaning in concert, and rocking their bodies in sympathy.

Suddenly he yelled out, "Ah! there it is; see there, see there; there he goes into the fire, the miserable lizard, which was purposely put into Tina's drink, and has grown in her, and poisoned her blood until I came to drive it out!"

Every one jumped to see the lizard, and saw nothing but the glowing logs. There was a faint smell of burning flesh. The women fell back into their seats, staring fearfully into each other's faces. Tina sprang upright in bed.

"Min is down by the Black Run calling me, an' I'm goin' to her. He told me to put her hair and some stuff he

give me into a hole in the black-gum
that hangs over the stone, and I did it.
Before God! I never meant to hurt her.
I hated her because Marse thought more
of her than he did me. He taught her,
but he never taught me, and we was both
his children. But I never meant to hurt
her. Tell Religion so. I'm comin', Min;
yes, I'm comin'; wait for me!"

She leaped upon the floor, but the unnatural strength supplied by the delirium
of fever had fled. She dropped at Religion's feet with a cry like a wounded
dog.

Daylight found Religion in the lonely
swamp: only great pools of thick black
water and leaning trees shrouded in long
gray moss. The water lay still in those
levels until the sun dried it up. In just
one place was there the slightest movement. A short descent sent a stream
slowly curling away under masses of
green briers.

The only stone known to be in the
whole swamp was at the head of the
stream, on a tiny hillock formed of logs
and the débris of many freshets. It was
known as Cuffee's Stone, and the story
was that a slave escaping from his master, and hiding in the swamp, had carried
the stone there to build his fire upon.

Close by, its sprawling roots washed by the running water, was an immense black-gum, in the branches of which the same Cuffee had built himself a covert of branches, from which he watched his pursuers in their vain hunt for him. Had Cuffee's shade, which was said still to haunt the tree, been abroad at that hour, it would have seen a girl narrowly scanning the rough stem, to find some crack or cleft in which anything might be hidden.

And she found a small crevice which would have escaped any but her searching eyes. They lit up as if she had found a rare treasure. Inserting the point of a knife, she drew out a little bag wet and mouldy. She never stopped to examine it, but leaped from log to log through the briers and water out of the swamp.

"Here's your hair, Min. Curl it round your finger three times and throw it in the fire. Oh, Min, now youna'll get well!"

A light shone in the sick girl's eyes. "Yes, I shall get well. Come out and listen to the music, Religion."

"There isn't any music, Min. See the hair."

"Yes, I see the hair; but, oh, the beautiful music! If I could only learn it!"

Religion clasped her close in her arms.

The water-oaks were in a golden-brown
haze, and the room was full of rich light.
But it swam in darkness before the exhausted girl.

A moment after she recovered herself,
but Min was well.

The Reprisal

BY H. W. MCVICKAR

I

IT was the 17th of March, yet the sun shone brilliantly, and the air was soft and balmy as on any July day. Even the good St. Patrick could have found no possible cause for complaint.

Most of the invalids about the hotel had ventured forth upon the terrace, and sat in groups of twos and threes basking in the sunshine. Their more fortunate brethren who were sojourning merely for rest after the arduous duties of a social season had long since taken themselves off to the pursuits best suited to their inclinations and livers.

One exception, however, there was to this general rule. A young man of some thirty years of age, who, seated upon the first step of a series leading from the terrace to the road, semed quite content

to enjoy the warmth and sunshine in a
purely passive way.

To some of those seated in their in-
valid-chairs it seemed as if he had not
moved or changed his position for hours,
and after a while his absolute repose
rather irritated them.

Nevertheless, he sat there with his elbows resting on his knees and a cigarette
between his lips. The cigarette had long
gone out, but to all appearances he was
blissfully unconscious of the fact.

A pair of rather attractive eyes were
gazing into space, and at times there was
a fine, sensitive expression about his lips,
but the rest of his features were commonplace, neither good nor bad. His
face being smooth-shaven gave him from
a distance a decidedly boyish appearance.

There was something, however, about
him which might be termed interesting,
something a trifle different from his
neighbors. Even his clothes had that
slight difference that hardly can be explained.

After a while his attention was drawn
to a very smart-looking trap, half dog
and half training cart, which for the past
fifteen minutes had been driven up and
down by the most diminutive of grooms.
Slowly he took in every detail, the high-

actioned hackney, the handsome harness,
the livery of the groom, even the wicker
basket under the seat with its padlock
hanging on the hasp. Lazily he attempted to decipher the monogram on the
cart's shining sides, but without success.
Five minutes more passed, and still up
and down drove the groom. Was its
owner never coming? he thought. Surely it must be a woman to keep it waiting
such a time. Little by little he became
more interested in the vehicle, and inci-
dentally in its mistress, and he found
himself conjecturing as to what manner
of person this was. Was she tall or short,
fat or lean, good figure or bad. On the
whole, he thought she must be "horsy."
That probably expressed it all.

How long these conjectures would
have lasted it would be hard to say, had
not just then the owner of the trap and
horse and diminutive groom herself put
in an appearance. She came out of the
hotel entrance drawing on one tan-color-
ed glove about three times too big for a
rather pretty hand. She wore a light-
colored driving-coat which reached to
her heels, and adorned with mother-of-
pearl buttons big enough to be used for
saucers. As she passed down the steps
he had a good opportunity to take her in,

and when she stopped to give the horse
a lump of sugar, a still better chance for
observation was afforded.

He could hardly say whether she was
good-looking or not; he was inclined to
think she was. She had a very winning
smile—this he noticed as she gave some
instructions to the groom. On the whole
his verdict was rather flattering than
otherwise, for she impressed him as being decidedely smart, and that with him
covered a multitude of sins.

At last she took up her skirts and
stepped into the cart, gathered up the
lines, and drew the whip from its socket.
The groom scrambled up somehow, and
after a little preliminary pawing of the
air, the horse and cart, driver and groom,
disappeared down the road.

"Hello, Jack! What are you doing
here sitting in the sun? Come along
and have a game of golf with me."

"Thanks! By-the-bye, do you know
who that young woman is who has just
driven off?"

"Certainly; Miss Violet Easton, of
Washington; very fond of horses; keeps
a lot of hunters; rich as mud. Would
you like to know her?"

"Yes. Much obliged for the information. Oh, play golf? No; it's a very

overrated game; you had better count
me out this morning."

An hour later, when she returned, had
she taken the trouble to notice, she would
have seen him still sitting at the top of
the same flight of steps, seemingly absorbed in nothing.

II

Three weeks had now passed since that
17th day of March, and Jack Mordaunt
had been introduced to Miss Easton; had
walked and driven with Miss Easton;
had ridden Miss Easton's horses to the
hunt three times a week—in fact, had
been seen so much in the society of the
young woman that gossips had already
begun to couple their names.

If, however, Miss Easton and Mr. Mordaunt were aware of this fact, it seemed
in no wise to trouble them, nor to cause
their meetings to be less frequent. A
very close observer might, if he had
taken the trouble to observe, have noticed that on these various occasions
Miss Easton's color would be slightly ac-
centuated, and that there was a perceptible increase in the interest she was wont
to vouchsafe to the ordinary public. But

then there were no close observers, or if there were they had other things to interest them.

On this particular day — it was then about 2 P.M. — Jack Mordaunt leaned lazily against the office desk, deeply absorbed in the perusal of a letter. The furrow that was quite distinct between his eyes would seem to indicate that the contents of the same were far from agreeable.

Twice already had he read the epistle, and was now engaged in going over it for the third time.

He was faultlessly attired in his hunting things, this being Saturday and the run of the week. Whatever disagreeableness may have occurred, Jack Mordaunt was at least a philosopher, and had no intention of missing a meet so long as Miss Easton was willing to see that he was well mounted. His single-breasted pink frock-coat was of the latest cut, and his white moleskin breeches and black pink-top boots were the best that London makers could turn out. His silk hat and gloves lay upon the office desk beside him.

" You seem vastly absorbed in that letter, Mr. Mordaunt; this is the second time I have tried to attract your attention, but with little success. I trust the contents are more than interesting."

Jack whirled round to find himself face to face with Miss Easton. Try as he would, the telltale blood slowly mounted to his tanned cheeks, suffusing his entire face with a ruddy hue. Instinctively he crumpled up the letter in his hand and thrust it into his coat-pocket, then, with a poor attempt at a smile, answered her question. "Yes; the letter contains disagreeable news, at least so far as I am concerned. In fact, I will have to return to New York Sunday morning."

"But you are coming back?"

He shook his head. "I fear it will be 'good-by.'"

Did he observe the quiver of her lips? Perhaps so. Still, no one would have known it as he stood there, swinging his hunting-crop like a pendulum from one finger.

And she—well, the quiver did not last long, and with a little laugh and shrug she continued: "I suppose most pleasant times come to an end, and perhaps it is better that they should come too soon than too late. But, Mr. Mordaunt, we must be going—that is, if we are to be in time for the meet."

" Where is it to be ?"

" At Farmingdale, and that is twelve miles away."

Together they walked down the wide corridor, and many an admiring glance was bestowed upon them as they passed, and many an insinuating wink and shrug was given as soon as their backs were turned.

Together they passed through the hotel door on to the terrace and down the steps—those same steps upon which Jack Mordaunt had sat just three weeks ago and watched her drive away. There was the same trap waiting, the same diminutive-looking groom standing at the horse's head. He helped her in, a trifle more tenderly, perhaps, than was absolutely necessary. Then he mounted to the seat beside her, and away they drove, the groom behind hanging on as by his eyelids.

All during those twelve miles they talked together of anything and everything, save on the one subject which was uppermost in their minds. Religiously they abstained from discussing themselves, and yet they knew that sooner or later that subject would have to be broached. Instinctively, however, they both avoided it, as if in their hearts they knew that from it no good could come.

At Farmingdale, as they drove into the stable-yard behind the little country tavern, all thoughts but of the hunt were banished, at least for the moment. They were both too keen about the sport not to feel their pulses quicken at the familiar scene and sounds.

All the hunters had been sent over in the morning, and stood ready in the adjoining stalls and sheds; grooms were taking off and folding blankets, tightening girths and straps preparatory to the start. In the middle of the stable-yard, O'Rourke, the first whip, was struggling with all his might and main to get into his pink coat, which had grown a trifle tight, and was giving the finishing touches to his toilet, gazing at himself in a broken piece of looking-glass that a friendly groom was patiently holding up before him.

Gentlemen and grooms were going and coming, giving and receiving their final instructions. The baying of the hounds, and the dashes here and there of color from pink coats, all went to make up a most charming and exhilarating picture.

Into the midst of this noise and bustle came Miss Easton and Jack. The groom scrambled down from his perch, and the two got out. In an instant she was surrounded by three or four men, all talking at the same time and upon the same subject: "Was not the day superb?" "Did she know which way the hounds were to run?" "Was she going to ride Midnight?" "What a beauty he was!" and a great deal more of the same kind.

She was gracious to all, and when at last Jack returned, followed by a groom leading her horse, not one man of that group but felt that Miss Easton was simply charming, and any one who married her was indeed in luck.

Jack stood aside to let young Martin give her a lift into the saddle, and watched him somewhat wistfully as he arranged her straps and skirt. At the final call every one sought his horse, mounted, and away they went, chattering and laughing.

The run was one of the best of the season, and after it was over Jack found himself riding by Miss Easton on their homeward journey.

Perhaps the others had ridden quite fast, or perchance these two had gone at a snail's pace, but when half-way home they looked about them and found that they were alone.

As far as the eye could reach along the wooded road no living thing was to be seen. The sun was setting like a globe of fire, and the red shafts of light penetrated between the straight trunks of the tall trees, bringing them out black against the evening sky, while the soft breeze moaned through their branches laden with the odors of hemlock and pine.

And this was the end. Another twenty minutes and the hotel would loom up before them, and the little farce, comedy, or tragedy, whichever it might be, would be finished. The curtain would fall, and the two principal actors would disappear.

No art could have given a finer setting to this the last act.

Neither cared to break the spell, and so they rode in silence until it seemed as if the intense stillness could no longer be borne. It was she who first spoke:

" And so it is really good-by ?"

For a long time he did not answer, but gazed steadily ahead of him, looking into space.

" Yes," he said at length, " it is good-by; and it were better had it been good-by three weeks ago."

" Why ?"

He gave a little start, merely repeat-

ing the word after her in a queer absent-
minded way.

"Yes, why?"

"Oh, I don't know."

Again silence fell upon them both.

"Violet," it was the first time he had
ever used that name.

Violet Easton turned in her saddle
and looked straight at him, trying to
read something in those dreamy eyes.
He met her gaze quietly.

"Why do you call me Violet?"

"Because—because—" He drew in his
breath sharply, and hesitated.

"Because—" and she looked inquiringly in his face.

"Don't ask me; please don't ask me. I
believe I am mad."

Again she let her eyes rest upon him
with the same earnest look of inquiry.

He turned away, and gazed absently
into the trees and underbrush.

In a few minutes she again spoke. "Is
this all you have to say, especially—especially "—and she paused a moment as
if searching for a word—"if this is the
end?"

Again he turned and looked at her.
Their horses were now walking side by
side, and very close; one ungloved hand
lay upon her knee.

10 S. H. D.

He leaned over and took it, and attempted to draw her towards him.

"No, no, not that; please not that."

"Why?"

"Can't you see—can't you understand? You and I are going to part—this very night, in fact, and—and— Oh, please do not."

He paid little heed to what she was saying, but drew her closer to him. The blood rushed to her cheeks, suffusing them with a deep red glow. Nearer and nearer he drew her, until, half-resisting, half-willing, her lips met his. It was but for an instant, and then all was over. She drew herself away from him, and the blood faded from her face until it was very white. Two tears welled up into her big blue eyes, overflowed, and ran down her cheeks.

"Oh, why did you do it? Otherwise we might have remained friends. But now," and she looked him fair in the face, while her words came slowly and distinctly, "you belong to me, for you are the only man that has ever kissed my lips."

A little shiver passed over Jack as he heard her speak. He could find no explanation for the feeling.

The next day Miss Easton found on her

plate at breakfast a big bunch of red roses. Attached to them was a card, and on it the single word "Adieu!"

III

A month later Violet Easton sat at the writing-desk in her little private parlor. Her elbows were on the table, and her head rested on her hands. Scalding tears were in her eyes, and try as she would they forced themselves down her cheeks. Before her lay a letter, which she had read for the twentieth time.

It was a simple, commonplace note at best, and seemed hardly worthy of calling forth such feeling. It ran as follows, and was in a man's handwriting:

"MY DEAR MISS EASTON,—Remembering that you told me you expected this week to run up to New York, I write in behalf of my wife to ask if you will give us both the pleasure of your company at dinner on Thursday evening.

"If you like, we can go afterwards to the play.

"How is Midnight, and is he still performing as brilliantly as ever?

"Sincerely,   J. MORDAUNT."

At last, with a great effort, she stopped her tears, and wiping her eyes with her soaking handkerchief, drew out a piece of note-paper from the blotter and began to write.

The first three attempts were evidently failures, for she tore them up and threw the pieces into a scrap-basket; the fourth effort, however, seemed to prove satisfactory.

"MY DEAR MR. MORDAUNT, — Many thanks for your and your wife's kind invitation. I have altered my plans, and no longer expect to go to New York.

"Midnight is a friend I have never found wanting.

"Very sincerely,   VIOLET EASTON."

She read this over carefully, folded, and placed it in an envelope. Upon it she wrote the name of John Mordaunt, Esq., and the address, and ringing a bell, delivered the letter to a hall-boy to mail.

Long after midnight she was still sitting there, gazing seemingly into space.

Jack Mordaunt looked for an instant at the calendar which stood in front of him upon his office desk.

In large numbers were printed 17, and

underneath the month of March was reg-
istered. He stopped writing for a moment. Somehow that date had forced
his mind back just one year, and as he
sat there he was going over again the
incidents of that time. They were all so
vivid—too vivid, in fact, to be altogether
pleasing. Had he forgotten Violet Easton? He had tried to forget her, but his
attempts were vain. Since they parted
he had never heard from or of her save
that one short note, and yet at odd intervals her remembrance would force itself upon his mind. Her parting words,
"You belong to me," haunted him.

And now, just as he was imagining that
the little incident was to be forever forgotten, that date had brought up freshly
and distinctly every detail of those three
weeks. After all, what had he done? A
passing flirtation with an attractive girl!
To be sure, he had omitted to say that he
was married, but, after all, it was not
absolutely necessary for him to proclaim
his family history to every passing acquaintance.

Somehow to-day the recollection of it
all irritated him. He felt out of sorts and
angry with himself, and inclined to place
the blame on others. He shrugged his
shoulders and went on with his work.

He would dismiss it all now and forever, and yet, try as he would, it would persist in coming back.

He threw down his pen and left the table, going over to the window. The outlook was far from encouraging, the March wind blew in eddies along the street, and now and then the rain came down in sheets, so that the opposite buildings were hardly visible. He shivered slightly; the room felt cold. He went back to his desk and rang the bell. One of the clerks answered it at once.

"Jones, I wish you would turn on the steam heat. The room seems chilly."

"Sorry, sir, but the steam is on full blast. Is there anything else that you wish?"

"No; you can go."

He sat down, and for the next hour again tried to concentrate his mind upon his work. It seemed useless. He looked at his watch; it was a quarter to six. "I think I will have to go home," he muttered to himself. "I don't feel very well, somehow."

John, the office-boy, here put in an appearance. "I beg pardon, Mr. Mordaunt, if you don't want me any more to-night, may I go? All the other clerks have gone."

" Yes." And John disappeared into the
outer office.

A few minutes later he again put in his
head. " Mr. Mordaunt, a lady wishes to
see you; shall I show her in ?"

" Certainly."

The door was flung open, and Violet
Easton entered.

So sudden and unexpected was her appearance that Jack had to grasp the desk
to steady himself. Really, he thought,
my nerves must be frightfully unstrung.
I think I must take a holiday. Aloud,
he said: " Why, Miss Easton, this is a
most unexpected pleasure. Won't you be
seated ? Can I be of any service to you ?"

He drew a chair up for her, and she
took it, and he sank back into his own.

And now for the first time he had an
opportunity to look at her, for she had
pushed up the heavy veil that covered
her face.

She looked ghastly white, and heavy
black rings were round her eyes. " Miss
Easton, you look ill. Can I get you anything ?"

" Oh no. I am not ill."

He said no more, but waited for her to
speak. At last she did. " Mr. Mordaunt,
I thought a long time before troubling
you, but I decided that as it was purely a

matter of business you would not object.
I desire you to draw out my will, and, as
I am contemplating leaving the city to-
morrow, it would be a great convenience
if you could do it now and let me sign it.
Then perhaps you would be good enough
to keep it for me. I have my rea-
sons—"

"I can assure you that I shall be more
than pleased to do anything you request."

"Then will you kindly write as I dic-
tate? Of course I wish you to put it
in legal form, as," and she smiled, "I
prefer to avoid litigation."

He drew towards him several sheets of
legal cap, and began to write as she dic-
tated.

He read it over to her when it was finished, and she nodded approval.

"And now, if you will execute it, I will
try and get the janitor and his wife to acknowledge the instrument. I regret to
say all my clerks have gone home."

He got up and left the room, returning
in a short time with the janitor and his
spouse. Miss Easton took the pen from
Jack's hand and wrote her name, Violet
Easton, in a clear, distinct manner. The
janitor subscribed his name as one of the
witnesses, and his wife did the same.

Jack thanked them both for their
trouble, and they departed. He took the
document, and having placed it in an
envelope, sealed it with his own seal, and
put it away in the safe.

"I don't know how I can thank you,
Mr. Mordaunt. If you will kindly send
your account to me in Washington, it
will be paid."

Jack protested. "I could not think of
taking any pay for such a trifling service, I assure you."

"Yes, but if I insist?"

"Oh, very well; I will do as you wish."

"And now I must be going." She
rose from her chair and began drawing
on her gloves, while he sat and watched
her. Suddenly an irresistible desire seemed to take possession of him. A desire in
some way to make amends for the past.

He pushed back his chair and stood
facing her. Several times he attempted
to speak, but no sound would come from
his parched and burning lips. He stretched forth his hand and took her ungloved
one, the same as he had done a year ago.
It seemed to him that it was icy cold.
Again he tried in vain to say something.
Slowly he drew her close, still closer to
him, until their lips again met in one
long kiss.

Her lips were cold, while his were burning hot. It seemed a long, long time before she gently disengaged herself from his embrace. A sweet smile flitted across her pale face.

"Yes," she said, as if speaking to herself, "this is the second time, but it will be the last. And now I must be going. Adieu!"

He went with her into the hall and down to the elevator, and saw her into the cab. He forgot to ask her where she was staying. His brain seemed to be on fire.

The next morning he felt far from well, and at the breakfast-table his wife remarked upon his looks.

"Oh, it's nothing, dear; I think I am a little overworked. As soon as I can dispose of the Farley case I shall try and get away, but it is too important to leave before it is decided. Is there any news in this morning's paper?"

"Nothing very startling, except I see the death of your friend Miss Easton, in Washington."

"What!" Jack fairly grasped the table for support. "Impossible! There is some mistake." He was now deathly white.

"Perhaps there is some mistake; but

here is the notice," and she handed him
the paper.

Hurriedly he ran his eye along the
death notices until he came to this
one:

"EASTON, VIOLET.—On the 17th day of
March, at the residence of her father, K
Street, Washington, of diphtheria, aged
twenty - three years. Notice of funeral
hereafter."

For some time he sat there as if
stunned, until his wife broke in upon his
thoughts.

"It seems to me," she said, "that you
take this matter very much to heart."

He did not answer her, but soon ex-
cused himself, and left the table.

He went straight to his office and into
his private room. With trembling fingers he made out the combination of the
safe, and opened the heavy iron doors.
There, where he had placed it the night
before, lay the sealed envelope. Beads
of perspiration stood out upon his forehead, and he was shaking like an aspen
leaf. Surely, he thought, I must be ill
or mad. He took the envelope and tore
it open; his hands were trembling so
that he found it difficult to unfold the
document. There, at the bottom, in her
clear handwriting, was the signature of

Violet Easton. There, also, were the sig-
natures of the janior and his wife. In
feverish haste he read the will. It was
just as he had written it the night before.
It left all her money to her father with
the exception of a few gifts.

Midnight had been left to him. He
remembered protesting, but she had told
him that she was sure he would always
be kind to the animal.

He rang the bell, and John appeared.

"Did you show a lady in here last
night just before you went home?"

"No, sir."

"Are you positive?"

"Yes, sir."

"Go and get the janitor, and tell him
I wish to speak to him."

In a few minutes that dignitary put in
an appearance.

"Is that your signature?" and Jack
handed him the will.

"Yes, sir; I signed it last night at your
request, and so did my wife."

"Was there a lady here at the time?"

"No, sir."

Jack put his hand up to his forehead.
"My God!" he muttered, "I must be
going mad." Suddenly everything began
to whirl about him, and he sank exhausted into his chair.

"John," he said, "send for a cab; I am feeling very ill, and must go home."

Four days later he was dead. The family doctor pronounced the case one of malignant diphtheria.

THE END

www.ingramcontent.com/pod-product-compliance
Lightning Source LLC
Chambersburg PA
CBHW030342020726
47493CB00003B/646